A YOUNG MAN'S FANCY

M. Tasia

Susan Mac Nicol

Emily Mims

Kitty Bardot

Elle Wright

www.BOROUGHSPUBLISHINGGROUP.com

PUBLISHER'S NOTE: This is a work of fiction. Names, characters, places and incidents either are the product of the author's imagination or are used fictitiously. Any resemblance to actual events, locales, business establishments or persons, living or dead, is coincidental. Boroughs Publishing Group does not have any control over and does not assume responsibility for author or third-party websites, blogs or critiques or their content.

A YOUNG MAN'S FANCY
Copyright © 2021 M. Tasia, Susan Mac Nicol, Emily Mims, Kitty Bardot, Elle Wright

ISBN: 978-1-953810-55-7

A YOUNG MAN'S FANCY

DAVID

M. Tasia

Chapter One

"Over?"

"Yes. Over," Jeremy said without emotion as he began walking back to his new convertible, a graduation gift from his parents. David watched him go, standing alone on the curb in Brighton High School's parking lot. Students were calling out goodbyes, hugging, and saying, *I'll text you.* The school year was over, and it felt surreal.

"But why?" David asked as he tried to wrap his mind around their three-year relationship ending. "What did I do?" Maybe he could fix this.

Jeremy stopped mid-stride and spun around to face him. It was their last day of high school, and moments ago, David's biggest worry was going to college in the fall. Now everything seemed to hang in the balance.

"Listen, what we had was nice and all, but we're adults now and getting out of this backwoods town is my main concern. I want college to be my fresh start in every way," Jeremy said. He raised his arms wide, as if hugging the air. "I'm leaving myself open to new people and experiences." David's new ex had the nerve to wink. "I'm headed for Dallas next week to find an apartment. You didn't honestly think a high school romance would last past graduation, did you?"

"Hmm… Fresh start?" The words tasted like acid in David's throat. He didn't recognize this version of Jeremy. And what was wrong with high school sweethearts? His parents were. "Looks like you got everything figured out," David murmured. He was in shock and lucky he was still able to speak. This didn't make sense. They'd ridden in together that morning, as they always had, and everything was *normal*. Damn it. He didn't have a ride home. "You told me you loved me."

Jeremy closed the distance and placed his hand on David's shoulder. It felt cold and stiff. "I still do, only in a different way. You'll see, this is the right decision for both of us."

"Considering I haven't had a say in any of this, I doubt you know what is right for me." Now that the shock was fading, anger was moving in fast. David had coached Jeremy through his final exams only to facilitate his moving on.

"Don't be pissed off," Jeremy said while giving David a smile he'd once thought so sexy. Now it only made him even angrier. "Who knows, maybe there'll be a second chance for us somewhere down the road."

Really? David had enough self-respect to knock his ex's hand off his shoulder and said, "I doubt that. What would make you think I'd want anything to do with you after today's stunt?" He needed to be as far away from Jeremy as possible and turned around to leave.

"Wait. Don't you want a ride home?" Jeremy yelled, causing more than one student to turn in their direction. Great, their breakup will be all over social media in a matter of seconds.

"Not from you, asshole." David kept walking out of the parking lot and toward the main road. If he was lucky, he might be able to catch a ride home from his cousin, Gabe.

He passed his best friend, Jacob, standing on the sidewalk a few feet away from break-up ground zero. He looked mortified, but when he went to speak, David waved him off. Jacob would try to comfort him, and now wasn't the time. He wanted to rage for a while.

Jacob had warned him about Jeremy and had always said the day would come when David was no longer convenient, and Jeremy would dump him. Jacob had been right. He'd ignored his friend's warnings, not wanting to hear the warnings he must've known were truth somewhere deep inside. Ignorance was not bliss.

Everything around him blurred as his mind whirled with questions. His head hurt, and he felt like someone had punched him in the stomach. On autopilot, he made his way to the fire station. Anger, embarrassment, and the gut-wrenching pain of betrayal swirled through him as he struggled to keep his emotions under lock and key.

No way was he going to break down, at least not in public. Almost the entire time he'd been in high school, he and Jeremy had been a couple, a team, one constant he could be sure of besides his parents and Jacob. Now his certainty was torn to shreds along with his heart.

Why would Jeremy have kissed him this morning when David had hopped into the car if he intended to break up with him later in the day? Why give him a ride at all? Why would he keep up the pretense until the last few minutes of their final day of high school? The shit hadn't said a word about leaving next week until a few minutes ago.

David had never felt so gutted. His ex, on the other hand, wasn't torn up, or even showing remorse. He couldn't wait to get to Dallas and "experience" new people. Jeremy's attitude buried the knife deeper into David's back. They'd discussed college so many times over this last year, and never once had Jeremy given him a clue about his true plans. Plans he'd put in place while still leading David along while telling him he loved him.

Such bullshit.

He'd been played and was left to pick up the pieces while Jeremy jetted off to build this *new* life of his away from him and this town.

David loved Brighton. The small-town feel, the treelined streets, shops, and sense of community were the best. There wasn't anything wrong with small-town America, and Dallas held no appeal. Crowded streets, standoffish people, expensive rent, and anonymity. Busy people living *important* lives. Not. For. Him.

David planned on attending college right here in Brighton. He was following his dream to become a veterinarian. He'd gotten a part-time job at the local vet's office on the other side of town and volunteered at the animal shelter to gain more experience.

He growled at the memory of Jeremy repeatedly reassuring him they could make a long-distance relationship work. He'd been lying all along, telling David what he wanted to hear. He began rifling through his memories of the last six months, searching for any clue or a sign he may have missed, and found nothing. They'd been happy, making the breakup harder to accept.

His phone beeped for what had to be the tenth time since leaving, adding to the messages he was currently ignoring. Expected, but unwelcomed. The same voyeurism that had people stopping to look at car wrecks made people desperate to confirm the news about couples breaking up. As if his world hadn't been dragged out from under him, and he wanted to rehash the misery.

"Hey," a voice hollered. "Where you headed?"

David came out of his fog and looked up, realizing he was passing the fire station. His cousin Gabe was standing out front with his gym bag over his shoulder. David stopped and changed directions.

"Hey man," David replied. "You think you could give me a ride home?"

Gabe's brows lowered, and his eyes squinted. "Sure. Jeremy staying late at school?"

David didn't even stop to answer. He walked to his cousin's truck and waited outside the passenger door until he heard the click of the locks disengage and then hopped in. Gabe opened the driver's door and threw his bag in the back seat before getting behind the steering wheel. David didn't feel like talking and hoped his cousin wasn't looking for a conversation. All he wanted to do was go home and lock himself in his room until college classes started.

Mercifully, Gabe turned on the truck and pulled out onto Main Street without saying a word. As they drove, David watched the people walking along the sidewalks looking into storefronts. Some were laughing, a few were holding hands, while others smiled and waved at them as they passed.

How could everything go on as normal when his heart was breaking? Didn't these people know how horrible this day was? The sun was shining too bright, the sky too blue, and the people too happy. David doubted he'd ever be happy again.

Gabe turned right at the next set of lights instead of going straight to David's house.

"Where we going?" David asked while looking around.

"The Dairy Freeze," Gabe answered. "I feel like a milkshake."

"Funny, you don't look like one." It was an automatic response. They'd made lame jokes since David was a kid. Right now, he felt like he was going to be sick.

Gabe smiled wide. "There's the David I know."

"Sorry. It's been a rough day." Understatement of the century.

They pulled into the drive-thru, and Gabe rolled down his window and turned to him. "What do you want?"

David's stomach flipped. He didn't feel like eating. He didn't feel like doing anything. "I'm okay, thanks."

"Chocolate it is," Gabe stated.

David didn't bother to argue. Once the guy got something in his head, there was no stopping him, but he could try a different route. "Aren't Johnny and Lucy waiting for you at home." Everyone knew Gabe was crazy for his husband and daughter.

"Already texted I'd be late," Gabe answered as they pulled up to the speaker. "Two chocolate milkshakes, please."

"Huh?" David hadn't seen him take out his phone.

"While you were sitting in the truck, I shot out a text to Johnny."

They pulled up to the open drive-thru window to see their milkshakes waiting for them. Gabe handed over the cash, and while they were waiting for his change and the drinks, David noticed a shift change was in progress behind the Dairy Freeze's counter. Sure enough, karma wanted to mess with him some more.

"David." A girl he knew from chemistry class gasped like those actresses in the old black and white movies Grandma Rose liked to watch. Dramatic and overdone. "I'm so sorry to hear about what happened. That's horrible. You must be crushed. You need anything, text me."

Gabe handed him his milkshake and took his change but didn't say a word, allowing David to respond. Was he supposed to say thank you for her sympathy? He went with a nod, and thankfully they pulled away. David expected the questions to come hard and heavy, but again, Gabe said nothing.

David took a sip of his milkshake, and it tasted like sawdust. He set it down and stared out the window, not really seeing anything. What now? How did he go on when the person he loved didn't love him anymore? He felt like a wrecking ball had hit him. His sense of security and self was fractured. Who was he without Jeremy? Their lives had been intertwined for years.

Scenes played through his memories: last year's trip to the Grand Canyon, the basketball games, and the many dinners they'd shared at each other's houses with their families. Would Jeremy's parents still talk to him if they saw him on the street? Stupid questions assaulted him from all directions, and he couldn't come up with any answers.

"David?"

He turned to look at his cousin and realized the truck was no longer moving. They were parked outside of his house, and his parents' vehicles were gone. Perfect. He wouldn't have to sneak into his bedroom to avoid any questions. Yet, he didn't move. The empty house looked darker and colder than it had this morning.

Gabe turned off the ignition and sat back drinking his milkshake but didn't say a word. He didn't have to push David for the story. They both knew he'd talk. Gabe had been his sounding board since he was a kid.

"I want to disappear."

"Texas is a big state, so it's possible."

"Not big enough."

"That bad?"

"Worse."

"Understood. How long do you need to be gone for?"

"Until my classes start in the fall."

"I might be able to help you with that."

David turned in his seat to look at his cousin. "You're not even going to ask me what's happened?"

"Figured you tell me if you wanted to."

David huffed, knowing he'd spill, so he figured now was as good a time as any. "Jeremy broke up with me so he could go to college in Dallas, be a free man."

Gabe nodded but didn't reply.

"He waited until the end of the last day of school to tell me about his plans. He's leaving for Dallas next week to find the perfect apartment for his new life. Didn't give me any hint it was coming. I thought we were great together. Asshole."

"I agree, that's pretty low."

"It's like I don't matter and never did. I was a convenient boyfriend for high school. I feel used. You should've seen him, all *starting a new life with new experiences and new people*. He wasn't broken up about it. Three years wasted. I'm an idiot."

"You're seventeen. Nothing you've done so far is time wasted. And you're far from being an idiot."

"It still hurts, and I'll be eighteen this summer."

"True, a broken heart doesn't care how old the person is."

"So, what do I do now?"

"I can't tell you that. The pain is too raw for you to listen to good sense, and anything I say won't matter. You have to deal. Though, it's not a bad idea to get away from Brighton to give you some perspective and space."

"I'm not going to a city, no way." He'd rather lock himself in his room, but he wasn't a child anymore.

"The place I have in mind has fewer people than Brighton, and it's only a couple counties over. Far enough, so you're not running into people daily telling you how sorry they are when all they really want is to rehash the details. Close enough you can come home and hang with your parents when you want."

David thought about the offer. "What would I be doing?"

"An old friend is renovating a lake house over on Fire Lake. He could use the extra help, and there are plenty of rooms you can bunk in."

"Who is he?"

"His name is Brick. He's a retired Navy Seal who inherited the house from his great aunt. He's cool, and he needs the help. You can spend two months on a lake repairing a house while you repair yourself. It'll give you the chance to get your head straight."

David looked around his front yard at the flowerbeds Jeremy helped him build over a long weekend and the freestanding birdhouse they'd been forced to make in shop. He wondered what Jeremy was doing right now.

Any other day they'd be inside playing video games or watching television until Jeremy had to leave for dinner.

David knew he was being pathetic, but he felt like even his home had turned on him.

"I'll do it."

Chapter Two

Well, it wasn't too bad. David was the type—going to be a vet, remember—who enjoyed fighting a raccoon in his blankets and dodging water spiders while repairing a dock. He drew the line at being swarmed by mayflies every time he went outside. July in Texas, and living next to a lake, bugs ruled. He'd been at the lake house for a week, and more things with pinchers had bitten him than he'd imagined existed. Along with itchy red bumps, he'd scraped a good portion of his hands and knees trying to fit under the house in search of a leaking pipe.

What the hell had his cousin been thinking sending him to this place? He hadn't stopped working since he got here. Lieutenant Commander Brick was a hard-ass all the time. Like he was back in SEAL training and David was a new recruit. His body ached all over, but he'd be damned if he'd give up and return to Brighton. It'd become a matter of pride to survive the summer and stay for the duration as he'd *sworn* when he arrived.

Yep, the crazy ex-Navy SEAL made him swear in front of Gabe to stay for exactly sixty days. It felt like he'd entered BUD/S. When he asked the guy what his last name was, Brick stated it wasn't necessary. The *La Vida Loca* tattoo across Brick's chest, wasn't false advertising. Navy Seals had a reputation for being a touch insane, and Brick was a prime example. Currently, he was clearing the front yard so Brick could have a Dumpster delivered before renovations began. Lumber would be arriving mid-week, and Brick needed a clearing for that as well.

The weed-whacker he'd been given died over a half-hour ago, unable to keep up with the ass-high grass. Brick had brought him a replacement tool. A newly sharpened hand-held sickle he'd found in what was left of the shed. Hell, now he resembled Van Gogh's *Peasant with Sickle*. He wondered if he recommended bringing in a herd of goats to clear all the brush how Brick would react.

As he hacked away, David often came across an odd thing or two buried in the grass: a garden gnome, a birdfeeder, a rainbow-colored turtle, two concrete chipmunks, a tire, and a complete set of wrought-iron garden furniture. He set everything off to the side so Brick could decide what he wanted to keep.

Even though he'd only been away for a short time, David missed home. His parents and his mom's cooking, for sure, but most of all, he missed his friend Jacob. Up until now, he hadn't realized how big a part Jacob was in his daily life.

They used to talk several times a day during school, meet up at the diner for fries, or to hang out and play video games. They'd known each other since kindergarten, shared every scraped knee, grounding, and accomplishment. David was feeling guilty for bugging out like he did. He'd texted and told Jacob where he was going and why, but he hadn't had the balls to talk to his friend, even though he knew Jacob wouldn't judge him. He'd have to make it up to him when he returned to Brighton where his best friend would be attending college too.

By three in the afternoon, David cut his last clump of grass and raked up the clippings into multiple paper compost bags, which had created a wall by the time he'd bagged the last of the debris He was dirty, itchy, and sweaty, and was dying to take a cold shower.

As if Brick had read his mind, he turned and said, "Why don't you go for a swim, and then we'll have barbeque burgers for a late lunch?"

"Really," he asked. "You sure there isn't something else you want me to chop, crawl under, tear down, or chase out of the house?"

The SEAL grinned. "Don't tempt me."

David dropped his sickle and took off at a run for the house before Brick changed his mind. It took no time at all to ditch his dirty jeans and t-shirt, change into his swim trunks, dash out of the house, and take a running jump off the newly repaired dock into the cool, fresh water. When he surfaced, he floated onto his back and stared at the clear Texas sky as the sun's rays beat down on everything it touched on this steamy summer day. After drifting peacefully for what seemed like a few short minutes, a clang sounded and he looked up to find Brick standing on the wrap-around porch striking a large metal triangle like they'd used in old westerns. Apparently, lunch was ready.

Shaking himself out on the beach before going over to the table and chairs got rid of most of the water. He used the towel Brick threw at him to take care of the rest. He glanced over at the burgers on the grill, and the sweet tea and chips sitting on the table. Brick motioned to the house, "Before you get a plate, there's a surprise inside you need to check out."

David couldn't imagine what the SEAL thought a surprise was. Probably a long list on the kitchen counter of jobs he'd have to complete in record time.

He threw the towel across the back of his chair, then turned around and grabbed it to put it in the hamper knowing Brick would say something about it later. The screen door slapped shut behind him, and he was sure it had left a mark on his ass when he stopped dead in his tracks. The person he'd wanted to see most was standing in the center of the living room.

"Jacob." The towel fell from his hand.

"Hey, buddy." Jacob grinned like he had a secret. His smile had always been mischievous.

"Oh my god." David ran across the room and wrapped his arms around his best friend, lifting him off the floor. "I missed you so much."

"Same." Jacob laughed as he hugged him back. "It was killing me not being able to hang with you every day. Are you okay?"

David held onto Jacob not willing to let him go. "Much better now. I have to tell you how sorry I am I didn't call you, but I'd been bummed and felt like an idiot for not seeing what you knew would happen."

"Hey. You don't have to apologize for feeling shit about a breakup. I'm sorry you had to go through it is all."

"Yeah, but you were so right. Jeremy dumped me the moment I didn't fit into his life plan. All this time, I've been a space filler until he moved on."

Jacob's expression hardened. "I would've rather been wrong. Don't let that asshole play on your worth."

David nodded. "Thanks for coming. You've always known how to make me feel better. How long can you stay?"

"You got me for as long as you want."

"You're here for the summer?" David couldn't believe what he was hearing. "Holy shit."

They both laughed making him feel lighter than he had in weeks. David grabbed Jacob's hand and dragged him outside. "I'm guessing," David said to Brick who was moving the platter of burgers to the table, "you two know each other."

Brick nodded when asked, as if it was NBD Jacob was here for the rest of the summer, "What do you two want to drink, water or sweet tea?" Brick lifted the lid to the cooler he kept on the porch.

"Two beers, please," David said nonchalantly.

"Come see me when you're both twenty-one."

"I'll have sweet tea." Jacob laughed.

"Buzz kill," David muttered.

"Hey, now. I've had my fun," Brick replied, grinning.

"Thanks for allowing me to come and stay here, sir," Jacob said as he grabbed a paper plate from the table.

"Who am I to refuse free labor?" Brick tilted up his chin to Jacob. "And call me Brick."

The three of them sat down on a set of plastic lawn furniture that had seen better days twenty years ago, but Jacob didn't seem to care. He kept glancing at David, a wicked glint in his eye as if he had a secret.

Brick poured them sweet tea, then silence reigned while they devoured their hamburgers without stopping to chat. David hadn't realized how hungry he was, and couldn't stuff food in him mouth fast enough. For the first time since Jeremy dumped him, he had a real appetite, and acknowledged the lead weight in his stomach had disappeared the moment he saw Jacob.

All evidence of their lunch was gone in minutes, and David was sitting back looking at the lake as a couple of boats in the distance crossed his sightline. He felt settled in a way he hadn't before and took a quiet moment to enjoy it.

The peace was shattered when the dilapidated shed gave up the ghost and came crashing down about ten feet from where they were sitting.

"Damn," David huffed.

"Chow time is over," Brick announced as he stood. "Back to it."

David pushed his stiff body to stand straight. "Do you ever rest?" Jacob chuckled.

"When I'm dead," Brick said.

"Cheery," David muttered.

"Determined," Jacob countered.

Brick grunted his assent. "Let's get on it. That shed isn't going to pick itself up."

"Save us," David said to Jacob, and they dutifully followed.

Chapter Three

August in Texas. A special kind of hell. Mercifully, the air conditioning in Brick's truck worked its magic in no time, stopping beads of sweat from rolling down David's back. He was on the road returning to the lake house from a run to the nearby town of Marshall, and its surprisingly well-stocked grocery store.

Today was his eighteenth birthday, and instead of waking up to an elaborate breakfast and well wishes, he was unceremoniously thrown the truck keys, handed a list, and shoved out the door. He knew Brick wasn't exactly a birthday party kind of guy. He'd probably be more comfortable jumping out of a plane than cooking up a pile of waffles, but David had hoped for some kind of birthday acknowledgment, especially from Jacob who hadn't even bothered to come out of his room before David left.

Over the past five weeks, Jacob had been by his side working his ass off, putting up with Brick's constant reminders of *this is how SEAL teams get things done*, so David couldn't be too upset with his best friend.

One night, a week after Jacob arrived, he'd come out of the house and found David sitting on the porch staring out at the water clutching his cellphone.

"What's up?" he'd asked as he plopped down next to David.

He turned the phone toward Jacob. "Jeremy texted."

"Huh. What'd he want?"

"Dunno. I erased the text and blocked his number."

The moonlight reflecting from the lake bounced off Jacob's white teeth, his smile was that wide. "'Bout fuckin' time."

David nodded. "Yeah, I think so too. I mean, it hit me hard when he dumped me, and I did the whole wallow thing 'til you got here. But, you know, we've been working side by side, swimming, hanging out, and it's been...easy. No pressure. The whole time Jeremy and I were together I always carried this weight worrying what he'd think if I did something with you and he wasn't included. Or, if I wanted to be alone, do my own thing, how he made me feel guilty for not wanting to be with him. At the time, I took it as love." He grunted. "Love shouldn't be a burden, and Jeremy was. I feel stupid for not realizing it a couple of years ago. Like I wasted all this time on someone who wasn't good for me."

"He's a charmer, and is a master manipulator. Don't beat yourself up for not seeing through him. He's good at it."

David shook his head. "You saw it, and tried to warn me."

Jacob put his warm hand on David's arm and squeezed. "Outside looking in is a whole lot easier."

David turned his body toward Jacob's and leaned in until they were only inches apart. "You're such a good person."

Jacob leaned in an inch closer. "So are you."

A thought popped David's mind: *all I have to do is dip my head and I could kiss him.*

Holy shit. Where did that come from?

To make sure he didn't do anything to ruin their friendship, David turned to face the lake, and that's when Jacob draped his arm over David's shoulder. Confused, but in a good way, he went with it. Having Jacob's arm around him felt so right, he leaned over and rested his head on Jacob's chest. His strong heartbeat thumping under his ear.

They sat like that until David shifted, and in unison they stood. Jacob took David's hand, and they went into the house and upstairs to their separate bedrooms, which didn't seem right. Like they shouldn't be sleeping separately.

Driving for over a half hour since leaving Marshall, David passed the gravel road to the lake house and had to double back. He wouldn't be sharing that miscalculation with Brick. As the truck bounced along the narrow road, which led to the three houses along the lake—they were so far apart he couldn't even see them unless he was swimming—he checked the time and saw it'd been over a couple of hours since he'd left. It wasn't even noon yet, but it was damn hot, and the bright sun piercing the windshield fought with the air conditioning for supremacy.

When he came to Brick's lane, he backed up the truck to sit parallel to house. He had five grocery bags he had a haul in sitting in the jump seat behind him and the passenger seat. Normally, he'd put everything in the truck bed, but it was too damn hot, and he didn't want anything to melt or go bad.

Hot as it was, he made sure to park under the shade of a large old tree, still it was unbearably hot as he headed for the passenger door. He slid all the grocery bags' handles onto his arms and shuffled to the back door, pulling open the screen with the edge of his shoe. He was setting his load down on the floor of the empty kitchen when his heart nearly came out of his chest.

"Happy Birthday, David," a number of people yelled, and then they began appearing from behind dining room furniture and from the living room. David was so shocked some of the grocery bags slid from his arms into a pile on the floor.

Along with Gabe, Johnny, and little Lucy, his mom and dad began singing happy birthday to him, while Brick and Jacob leaned against the kitchen wall with knowing grins.

No one had forgotten. They'd arranged a surprise party.

Balloons appeared from their hiding spots, and red streamers were placed on the old house's walls. A giant number "18" floated above them all, as his mom threw confetti at him while singing.

It was everything he'd wanted, but would never ask for. He should've known Jacob wouldn't let him down.

What an amazing day it'd turned out to be. They had a barbeque, his mom's homemade carrot cake with the super thick frosting, and tons of presents. All the great things that come with birthdays. They swam in the lake—they had to cool off something fierce—then they all sat on the porch as the sun slipped beneath the horizon.

"I can't believe you guys came all the way over here," he said to the group. "This has been the best birthday I could've ever imagined."

"Of course, sweetheart," his mom said. "We'd never miss something this important."

He should have known better.

"You look like you've grown over the summer," his dad commented. "Must be all the hard work." He swiveled his head to take in the house. "The place is looking good."

"David and Jacob have worked hard. You should be proud of them," Brick said.

Gabe held a sleeping Lucy against his chest, while Johnny had his hand wrapped around their daughter's ankle.

"It's certainly beautiful here," Johnny said. "So peaceful."

"You didn't see it when the grass stood a couple of feet tall, or when we battled two wasp nests for the porch." David laughed at the memory while slapping Jacob on the back. "Don't even get me going about the dock spiders and mayflies."

Jacob laughed. "I wouldn't want to be anywhere else."

"Hard work builds character," Brick stated.

"I must have a ton of character by now. Maybe I should change my major to acting, and forget about veterinary medicine."

The group laughed. He liked teasing Brick, though it took him a while to feel comfortable doing it. For all the tough guy attitude and indefatigable work ethic, the SEAL was a good guy.

Jacob leaned close to him and mock whispered, "I've seen your temper tantrums. You're a born actor if I've ever seen one."

More laughter, and David was warmed by his family's good humor.

"Well, we should go to get Lucy to bed," Gabe said as he stood. "Happy birthday, David, and thanks for having us out, Brick."

"Yeah, it's about that time," his dad said, following Gabe's lead. "Go get your bags, guys."

David wasn't sure what was going on and by the look on Jacob's face neither did he. "Our bags, why?"

"Brick said you guys have worked hard enough, and the two of you deserve a couple of weeks off before school starts. We're taking you home today."

David snapped his head around to look at Brick. "You're allowing me to leave two weeks early."

Brick nodded. "You've worked your ass off, kid. Happy Birthday. Go enjoy what's left of your summer vacation."

They could go home right now. Holy shit. It was what he wanted so bad he could almost taste it. Then why wasn't he running to his room to pack?

"Is something wrong?" his mom asked.

David looked between his parents, then to Brick and Jacob, knowing what he had to do but unsure if he wanted to force Jacob into it.

"I'm by your side stay or leave," Jacob said making David's decision easier. Seriously, Jacob was the best.

"Thank you for the offer, but when I came here, I gave my word that I would stay the sixty days. I'm not going back on my word." There was a slight uptick to the corner of Brick's mouth but nothing more to indicate how he felt about David's decision to stay.

"If that's what you have to do, son, then I respect that," his dad stated while giving him a heavy pat on his back.

"You're growing up so fast," his mom said before hugging him tightly. "We'll be back in two weeks to pick up you two. Jacob, we'll let your parents know you're doing well."

"Thank you, ma'am. Please tell them I miss them, and I'll see them soon," Jacob said. "They can call or text anytime."

David stood with Jacob watching his family's taillights fade into the distance, feeling good about his decision to stay. He knew Brick was the type of person who would never break his word and figured he'd do the same for him.

"Don't stay up too late. We're taking on whatever's moved in under the corner of the porch at sunrise." Brick's voice had them jumping. The man seemed to appear out of thin air.

"I'm going to put a bell on you, so you're not scaring the hell out of us all the time."

"Won't help," the SEAL said with a grin before walking away into the darkness.

Jacob looked at David and said, "Seriously cool move. You gotta wonder if he has to work at being mysterious and kickass, or if it comes naturally."

They walked into the lake house and David headed straight for the kitchen for a drink of water. Thirst quenched, he went upstairs to Jacob's room and leaned against the door jamb. His friend was elbows deep in his bag, humming along to "Leave the Door Open." Every so often, he'd sway his hips in time to the music.

God, David loved watching him move and waited a few more moments taking in the show before asking. "Whatcha looking for?"

Jacob jumped, holding a small bag in his hand, and began laughing. "Man, I didn't hear you come in. You scared the hell out of me."

"Sorry. What's in the bag?"

"A surprise."

"For me?"

"Yeah. I got it for your birthday months ago but wanted to give it to you when we were alone."

Jacob handed the bag to David who looked inside at the small black box. "I'm guessing it's not a new car."

"Correct, genius" Jacob chuckled. "Open it."

David couldn't contain his smile as he dug out the box and flipped up the lid. He couldn't believe his eyes. Against a crushed velvet pillow was a gold chain with an amulet of the Veterinary Caduceus. It was an unbelievably perfect gift, and so like Jacob to think of it.

"I know you haven't graduated, or even started, but I have faith you will be the best damn vet in the state."

David's heart flipped and he pulled Jacob into his arms. "I love you, man."

Before he could become embarrassed about his outburst and back away, Jacob said, "Love you too."

Chapter Four

As they had since the day after Jacob arrived at the lake house, every afternoon they'd go for a swim, and every night they'd sit on the porch talking. Brick would usually disappear early, leaving the two of them alone.

Tonight was no different, as the moon rose high into the sky reflecting onto the calm lake. The occasional hoot from one of the area Eastern Screech, or Great Horned owls—David never got close enough to see which—and the rustle of leaves broke the silence as they sat staring out at the lake. Easy and comfortable, as it always was with Jacob.

As the days passed, David's feelings toward his best friend became stronger and clearer, but worried about how sharing what he felt would affect their friendship, he kept quiet about what'd been brewing in his heart. He didn't want Jacob to think he was a rebound, or that David was bouncing from one guy to the next.

No sooner than he had the thought, Jacob reached over and took his hand, entwining their fingers as he looked over at him, the question of what this meant written on David's face.

Excitement, happiness, joy all floated through him at the feel of Jacob's calloused palm in his. He squeezed their joined hands and said, "It's perfect."

After several long silent moments, Jacob said, "I don't want to pressure you. I know you've been through a lot these last few months, but I need you to know how I feel. I love you. I've loved you for years, and your being away brought it to a head. I was miserable without you. It was the roughest week in my entire life. I need you to know, but I don't expect anything in return."

David's heart was trying to pound its way through his chest wall, but he had to be rational. "I can't stand the idea of losing you and risking our friendship no matter how much I love you back, and I do. I love you as way more than a friend."

Jacob's blue eyes watched him carefully before he smiled. "For real."

"For absolute real. But, I won't act on it if it means I risk losing you as part of my life. That would kill me."

"I know what you mean. It's why I held back." His lips tilted up in that mischievous grin. "Here's what I think we should do. No jumping into anything. We know how we feel, and we don't want to lose our friendship. Let's take it as it comes and figure it out as whatever we have evolves. No pressure, no labels."

This was a big step, but the more David gazed into Jacob's eyes, the more right the whole thing felt. Most people dream of having a partner who was also their best friend. David couldn't ignore the emotions he felt for Jacob, and he didn't want to hide them.

He nodded. "Okay. Let's see what happens." David smiled and brought their entwined hands to his lips and kissed the back of Jacob's hand.

Jacob smiled, and they leaned closer to kiss for the first time under a full moon beside a lake where best friends began to explore how wonderful and natural it felt to taste each other's essence.

They sat hand in hand until the moon began to dip in the sky, and then they headed to their rooms. Leaning Jacob against the wall next to his bedroom door, David took one final kiss from lips he could get used to kissing good night for a long, long time. When they parted breathlessly, David went to his room and fell into bed happier than he'd ever been.

Yes, they were young, and anything could happen, but everything was right in his world, and he hoped he and Jacob would be able to achieve what so few people found.

A happy forever.

Together.

NO BUNNY LIKE YOU

Susan Mac Nicol

Easter could go suck eggs.

If Colin heard any more about the subject of the smooth, chocolaty oval treats, he'd throw up right over the screaming hordes of children who'd been following him around, giving him no peace. He supposed when one was the Easter Bunny, it was only to be expected.

Currently, Colin was tucked between the bushes on the right side of the park, hiding as best as he could being a gangly, five-eight human dressed in white, itching fur. Well, six-foot if you counted to the tips of his ridiculously furry ears. All courtesy of his interfering mother, Linda, who'd *volunteered* him this Easter Sunday for the task during the annual insanity of the ominously, and treacly named village event called, "The Hoppening." The parish of Cushing Downer in the county of Cambridgeshire hosted the event each year in the picturesque Northlake Park.

Colin delved deep down into his copious bunny suit pocket and produced a packet of cigarettes and a lighter. Taking a guilty glance around to check no one was watching— if his parents found him smoking, he'd be in for it— he lit one up and sighed in pleasure at the first inhale.

"The Hoppening," he muttered to himself. "Sounds more like a 'Children of the Corn' episode."

He smirked watching the group of three kids frantically searching for the Easter eggs he'd hidden around the grounds. His mother never said he should make it easy for them. He'd taken great creative pleasure in sourcing the riddles accompanying the hunt, steering the kids, he hoped, in the right direction, but not making it too easy. *After all, it was called a hunt for a reason, right?*

He took a drag of his cigarette and leaned back against the tree. It was a beautiful early April day, the sun was shining, the air breathed warmly against his skin, and all in all he supposed there were worst ways to spend his weekend.

He was however looking forward to his "Me Time" later this evening, which consisted of loitering by his bedroom window watching his neighbour's son mow the lawn, sunbathe in the front garden, or wash his father's car. It was his gay seventeen-year old's idea of heaven, fitting all the pop song stereotype videos he saw on the telly.

One of his favourites was Carly Rae Jepson's "Call Me Maybe." The hunk in that clip was radically sexy and formed the fodder for a lot of his jerk-off sessions. As did the gorgeous Dashiell Bailey next door.

Dashiell was dark-skinned—his West Indian heritage clear— with bouncing thick black hair, and deep brown eyes. When he took off his shirt, Colin's mouth grew dry at the broad shoulders, the perfect set of brown nipples, and the dusky trail of hair leading down into his baggy jeans. His voice was deep and husky, and Colin swooned whenever he heard it.

They were friends, sort of, if you counted the occasional BBQ 'round each other's houses, informal chats across the fence about school, mutual friends, and the state of the planet. Dashiell was passionate about helping developing countries, and was a staunch advocate of providing food and infrastructure for them.

"Hey, Mister Easter Bunny." Colin's fantasies were rudely interrupted by a three-foot urchin about four-years-old, with bright red hair, looking for all the world like an Annie. "You shouldn't be smoking. Mum says it's bad for you." The urchin's lips pursed in disapproval. "She says your insides will rot and turn black, and then when you poop, it will all come out into the toilet. Then you'll have to go to the ho'pital and they'll put a tube up your bum to get it all out." She blinked, her round, blue eyes serious. "I thought the Easter Bunny was supposed to be good."

Colin wasn't sure whether he was more disturbed a mother would tell her child such a gross story, or that it seriously made him think about quitting. He hadn't been smoking long so there was still time to give it up.

"Of course I'm good. I'm the Easter Bunny," he mumbled, spitting out fur that tickled his lips. "This is how I relax, and I don't do it often, so you needn't worry about me. Why aren't you hunting for eggs with the other kids?"

She frowned. "Because my brother Davy told me I was stupid because I couldn't read the clue. He told me to go play on the swings." Her face scrunched up like she was going to cry. God, please no crying. "But I want to find the eggs. I told my dad I'd bring him one back for dinner."

The urchin's face fell, and Colin wasn't such a cad that the sight of a sad little Annie didn't tug at his heartstrings. "Where's the clue, do you have it?"

Annie reached out a grubby paw and showed him a crumpled piece of white paper. "I stole it from him so he couldn't find the egg either." She gave a self-satisfied smile. "Here."

Colin took it and read it out loud. "This clue isn't up a mountain, but you'll find a delightful surprise over by the fountain." He looked down at her. "Well, that's not too hard. Do you know what a fountain is?"

She shook her head. "Nope." Her face grew hopeful. "Do you?"

Colin nodded. He crouched down and waggled his ears with his hand. "If you go over there, by the lake, there's a big stone lady with a jug on her shoulder. It's spouting water. That's the fountain. I think you might find something among the grass there." Providing no one else had already beaten her to it.

Her eyes lit up. "Ooh, really? Thank you, Mr Bunny." She wasted no time and scampered off. Colin sighed. He wasn't sure where her parents were and he didn't want any unfortunate accidents happening on his watch, like having a kid fall into the lake. He might not have volunteered to be the Bunny, but he took his job seriously.

"I suppose I'd better keep an eye on her," he muttered to himself. "If someone's taken her egg, then I can at least plant another one for her to find." He had a secret stash of marshmallow bunnies in his pocket. As Colin trudged across the park, waving to children and adults alike, and acting all happy to see the little ones running up to him and touching his fur, he noticed Dashiell cycling along the path alongside the park. His dream man had no shirt on—it was wrapped around his waist— and he had earphones in, no doubt listening to a mix of the electric dance music he seemed to love so much. Colin wasn't a stalker, but he may have had a vantage point from his bedroom into Dashiell's, if he twisted his body just so and hung over the window to the left a bit. Well, if he hung over quite a lot.

He'd seen Dashiell dancing around in his room, sexy body twisting and turning, bopping away to music coming from a speaker somewhere in his room. It was usually a mix of David Guetta, Calvin Harris, and Zedd. In his sillier romantic moments, Colin had dreamt of making Dashiell a mixed CD of music, but talked himself out of it as being too naff. After all, who did that for their next-door neighbour—a guy as well? Dashiell might punch his lights out because Colin had no idea of the other man's sexuality.

Colin was so busy side-ogling Dashiell, his burnished skin and impressive biceps, he didn't notice the Motability scooter barrelling towards him, or hear the driver's desperate shouts of "Watch out, there, you." He'd no clue how close he'd ventured to the lake's edge until he started falling, falling, and the icy wash of stale-smelling water closed over his head.

Then he began to sink to the bottom of the lake like a sackful of lead.

He flailed in panic, but the costume he wore was sodden and lay heavy on his body. Colin tried desperately to divest himself of the stupid costume but was dragged deeper into the murky depths.

I'm going to fucking die in a Bunny outfit and not the fun kind like in the porn mags. Holy shit, I'm gonna kill Easter.

He was already losing his breath, but it was more from panic. It seemed like minutes but had no doubt only been seconds when his feet touched the bottom of the lake. With a fervent thanks for shallow waters to the bunny gods above, Colin righted himself still under the water, and pushed off with his feet to reach the surface. He'd no sooner propelled himself a few inches up when strong hands gripped his waist and pulled, pulled, pulled until Colin's sodden headwear breached the waters. He gasped in relief as sunshine hit his eyes, and he no longer inhaled foul-tasting liquid.

"Here you go, mate. Safe and sound." The familiar voice turned Colin's insides all a flutter, and he groaned loudly as he wrenched the damn bunny head off and took a deep, rasping breath.

Of all the people to drag him out of his ignominious watery grave, it had to be Dashiell bloody Bailey.

Colin coughed and spluttered as his lungs made themselves known. "Thanks for the help," he rasped out as Dashiell's eyes widened in surprise.

"Oh, it's you," his neighbour exclaimed. "Bloody hell, mate. You chose a right time to go swimming in that get-up."

"It wasn't a conscious choice, "Colin snapped, suffused with embarrassment at having the man of his dreams not only see him in the bunny suit, but having a hand in his rescue. "Some old biddy on one of those fucking scooters shoved me in. Those people are a bloody menace."

"Those people," came a dry rejoinder from behind him, "yelled at you twice to move out of the bloody way." The imperious tones of Maggie Thatcher from down the road— yes that was her real name and the woman acted like the Iron Lady too. "And if you hadn't been so busy ogling this young man here," Maggie's gnarled fingers pointed at Dashiell, who grinned slowly, "perhaps, Mr Soaking Wet, you might not have ended up traumatising all these children who thought the Easter Bunny was dead."

Chuckles from all around echoed in Colin's ears, and he blushed scarlet as he turned to face the crowd that'd gathered. Snotty nosed, tearful toddlers, smiling parents, and a couple of Colin's old school mates sniggered at his predicament as the predictable mobile phones were raised recording his ghastly experience for posterity.

"Shit," he swore and Dashiell reached over and laid one calloused finger on Colin's lips.

"Uh-uh," he admonished with a twinkle in his eye. "There are kids present, Mr Easter Bunny."

Colin was pretty sure his heart palpitations were from his near-miss with death and not from having Dashiell's calloused finger lying on his lips. Or those burnt-caramel eyes gazing at him with both amusement and—was that affection?

"Sorry," Colin muttered, starting to shiver, because, well, he was drenched. "I think I need to get out of this suit and into dry clothes."

Dashiell nodded. "Don't let me stop you," he murmured. "Best to go somewhere private to do that, yeah? These kids have had enough excitement for the day."

Maggie snorted. "Smooth, Mr Bailey, very smooth." She shook her head, her grey-haired ponytail shaking from side to side. "Young Mr MacKenzie, I suggest you hurry home before you get pneumonia. And next time when someone tells you to get out of the bloody way—do so." She muttered something to herself and trundled off on her scooter. Around them, the crowd was dispersing, and Dashiell cocked a brow at Colin.

"I'll walk you home, make sure nothing else unfortunate happens to you.".." He eyed Colin appraisingly. "I'm guessing you have something else on under that thing? Best to get out of it. Not gonna be easy walking with that on." He motioned to a small clearing in the middle of the trees. "Let's go in there and sort you out. You need something a bit dryer, though. Hang on."

He approached a young couple sitting on the grass, and appropriated a picnic blanket, with his promise to return it to the park office when they were done with it.

Colin's teeth chattered as he followed Dashiell into the undergrowth. Soon they were hidden almost from sight and Dashiell tilted his head toward Colin.

"Ready to disrobe?" he asked with a cheeky grin. Colin's heart pitter-pattered so loud he was sure his sexy neighbour must hear it.

"Zips at the back," he stammered awkwardly. "Would you mind, uhm, unzipping me?" He closed his eyes in mortification. This wasn't the way he'd ever envisaged saying those words outside of a seduction scene where Dashiell would be all over him like a rash.

"Sure." Dashiell's voice had deepened. "Glad to oblige. Turn around."

Colin did, and closed his eyes as Dashiell stepped up behind up —his breath was warm against the back of Colin's neck, and unwilling goosebumps formed on his clammy skin—then the zip was drawn down to the base of Colin's spine, which tingled when Dashiell's fingers brushed his bare skin.

Colin stepped out of the costume, now clad in a pair of soaking wet skin-tight black jeans and a t-shirt that would have won any wet t-shirt competition. His nipples were stark against the fabric which clung to his stomach as if moulded on. He pulled it away with a grimace. His socks and plimsolls were as sodden, and he supposed moodily, the trudge home was going to be most uncomfortable.

He looked over at Dashiell, whose eyes dropped guiltily. Dashiell stepped away, and Colin thought he might have seen a touch of heat in those eyes. "Right," his neighbour said huskily. "Let's get this over you to warm you up. I'd give you my shirt, only it got wet when I went in to help you out. I forgot I had it around my waist." He grimaced. "I guess I should wear it now. Bare-chested in the park is one thing. I can't give everyone a glimpse of my bod in the public streets. There'd be a riot." He winked at Colin and shrugged into his wet sweatshirt.

Was he checking me out earlier? Colin wondered with a frisson of excitement. He may only be seventeen, but he knew a look of appreciation when he saw one. Well, well, well. Perhaps he did stand a chance with his hunky next-door neighbour after all.

Dashiell wrapped the thin cartoon-hedgehog emblazoned blanket around Colin's shivering shoulders. "There." He cleared his throat. "Not the best, but it'll hold you 'til we get back to yours."

I'd rather you hold me and warm me up, Colin thought longingly.

Dashiell gave Colin a chuck of his chin and grabbed his bike as he turned to start the walk home. "Come on," he said gruffly. "Let's get going."

Colin bundled the soaking wet costume up into his backpack which he'd secured among the bushes and hefted it onto his back. It weighed a ton but his mother would never forgive him if he abandoned it to the elements. She'd lose her deposit no doubt.

Sometimes it sucked being a good son.

***

The walk home was littered with the occasional clearing of a throat—both of them seemed to have a frog—a quick glance at each other, then an awkward smile as they looked away—and the sound of Colin's shoes as they squished wetly against the pavement. He tried to minimise the sound by placing his feet carefully as he trod, but the effort was making his calves ache. Of course, it was certain to happen, he managed to get a cramp crossing the pedestrian walk by their homes, and the sudden twist of his muscles, coupled with the onset of charley horse caused him to cry out in pain and bend down to rub his leg.

Dashiell stepped forward. "What's up?" he asked in concern. "Do you need any help? Maybe want to use the bike."

Given that Colin was gritting his teeth in agony and struggling to balance on one leg, he nodded. "No bike, thanks." That was all he needed. It had been a while since he'd ridden, and he'd likely fall off. "But if I could hold your arm until we get across?"

"Sure, mate," Dashiell said cheerfully. "Here you go. Grab away." He offered an impressive bicep to Colin who grabbed it as if were a life raft thrown from a sinking ship.

He couldn't help commenting as they reached the safety of the pavement on the other side. "Wow, you must work out a lot," Colin stammered, as he sank down gratefully onto the park bench by the old oak tree. He began to rub his calf again. "I'll never have muscles like you."

"Oh, I don't know about that," Dashiell said quietly as he sat down beside Colin, balancing his bike against the back of the bench. "I mean, you do all that callisthenics stuff, so I'd have thought you'd have a bit of a muscle on you by now."

"Callisthenics?" Colin squeaked. *What on earth is he talking about?* "Dashiell, I've never been to a gym in my life."

Well, he'd had a gym membership once, so he could do some circuit training, but after the second time his long legs had lost their footing on the treadmill and he'd collapsed in a heap on the floor. He had not gone back. Exercise + Colin did not a pretty picture make.

Dashiell's dark eyes twinkled as he sat back, laying an arm across the back of the bench, fingers brushing Colin's shoulders. "Call me Dash. Only my folks and my gran call me by my full name." He scrunched up his face adorably. "Oh, I thought all that stuff you did on the balcony at your place was some sort of exercise routine. I mean, it looks quite uncomfortable, you hanging over the rail like that, like a contortionist. I'd have thought you must be fairly flexible to get into those positions." His sly smile promised more teasing, and Colin wanted to run and jump back in the lake. Sink until the red heat on his face cooled down and he could crawl home without anyone seeing him.

Dashiell…Dash had noticed him spying. OMG. Colin needed to move. Right bloody now. Perhaps they needed people studying artificial intelligence in Outer Mongolia, or Alaska. He'd start researching as soon as he got home.

"Penny for them." Dash's amused voice interrupted Colin's plans to skip the country. "How's your leg feeling? Better?"

Colin avoided Dash's gaze as he stood up, wincing. "It feels better. I suppose, ermm, we'd better get walking again. I'm still damned cold." He marched down the road aware Dash was standing there watching.

A couple of minutes later Dash caught up and tapped Colin on his back. "Listen, I'm sorry if I made you uncomfortable back there. I was only having a joke."

Colin nodded haughtily. "No problem, I quite understand. I shall confine my callisthenics to my room from now on." He lifted his chin resolutely—and was shocked to hear Dash's loud chuckling.

"Wow, you are too adorable when you're in a snit. Did I say I didn't like your…uhm…unusual form of exercise? Did it occur to you that I danced in my room because I knew you'd watch me?"

Colin was still trying to get his head around the fact Dash had called him "adorable." That, and his stalking the boy next door was welcomed.

He stopped and narrowed his eyes at Dash, whose face reflected both a soft affection and a smirk. Colin wasn't sure he could ever pull off such a look. He'd probably look constipated.

"You mean you knew I was watching you all the time?"

Dash shrugged. "Well, not at first. Then there was that one day you almost fell off the balcony and had to pull yourself up. If I recall, you were in your underwear at the time." His grin widened. "I rather appreciated the sight, so I hoped you'd do it again sometime."

"What?" Colin said, aghast. "Fall off the balcony? You're quite the sadist, aren't you?"

Dash moved closer and suddenly Colin couldn't breathe properly anymore when those chestnut eyes bore into his. "I meant the underwear part. They were blue with yellow dolphins on them."

Colin's cheeks burned. He knew that piece of underwear intimately, of course, but he was mortified Dash had seen them.

"They were a special pair I bought to support the WWF and their 'Save the Dolphins' drive," he lied, because who the hell wanted to admit to owning something a five-year-old would wear? "My usual attire isn't as…uhm..colourful."

Dash nodded wisely. "Ah. Then the red pair with snowmen on them, they were for a good cause too, right? And the pink pair with the flamingos, did they do the trick? Supporting the Endangered Flamingo endeavour, I mean. I've always liked flamingos. It'd be a shame if anything bad happened to them." He walked ahead, chuckling and Colin wanted to swallow his tongue, choke himself senseless in embarrassment, then wake up being given the kiss of life by those, knowing, smiling lips.

Drat. This man is tricky. "You seem to pay a lot of attention to my underwear," he said loftily. "One could say you've been spying on me too."

Dash sauntered ahead, but looked back with a wicked glint in his eye. "Huh. I wondered when you'd spot that. I tried attracting your attention a couple of times, but you were always too busy with your, err, exercise routine."

"What?" Colin squawked as he rushed to catch Dash up. "How were you trying to do that? I didn't notice."

How could I have missed something like that?

Dash rolled his eyes and gave another one of his husky chuckles. "I waved you over a few times, I swung my hips your way, I even did the whole 'come hither' thing." He mimed the action sultrily, swinging his hips in time to the movement, leaving Colin's mouth dry and certain other parts of him aching. "But you never got the hint."

"I thought that was all part of your dancing routine," Colin said, wishing now he'd paid closer attention.

Dash shrugged. "I figured you were too shy. No worries, we're together now. That's all that counts."

Colin lost his breath. What the hell did that mean, together? Did he mean together, as in, they were, like, together, together, or did he mean they were in each other's company right now and nothing more?

Colin's brain hurt from the triathlon-like activity going on in there. Being seventeen was so fucking confusing sometimes. And, of course, now he wanted a smoke. Best have one before he got home. He stopped and looked around furtively. In the allotment they were walking past, over by old man Donovan's prize vegetable patch, was a small, open-framed garden hut with a bench where he liked to sit and watch his plants grow. Jed Donavan would sit smoking his foul-smelling cigars and regard his vegetables with a serene gaze worthy of a proud Captain looking over his sailing ship.

It would be the perfect out of the way place for Colin to have a sneaky ciggy.

He nudged Dash on the arm. "Follow me," he murmured and opened the creaking gate into the allotment, making sure no one else was there. *They're all at the egg hunt*, he thought. *We'll have a little privacy here for a bit.*

Dash looked intrigued. He sat his bike against the fence at the entrance, then followed Colin across the neat rows of daffodils, lettuce, spring onions, and irises, until they reached the hardy little hut. Colin sank onto the bench with relief, hoisting his backpack off, and massaging his shoulders, which had been rubbed a little raw with the weight of the wet bunny suit.

"That's better," he proclaimed as Dash sat beside him with a confused smile. "Time for one of these."

He drew out his packet of *emergency* cigarettes—there were only three in there—from his backpack, because, hello, the ones in his costume were of no use anymore, and lit up with a frisson of satisfaction. Colin took the first drag and his toes curled in pleasure.

"I didn't know you smoked," Dash said softly, eying the cigarette.

Colin scowled. "Please tell me you're not one of those anti-smoking people who preach to everyone about the health issues with this." He waved his ciggy, taking care not to send any smoke Dash's way. "I know it all already. My mum and dad are the worst. They're ex-smokers."

Dash shrugged one shoulder. "It's not a habit I like, but to each their own." His face shadowed. "I think alcohol is a worse offender. That shit breaks families. Generally, smoking only breaks the person doing it." He sounded as if he'd some personal experience with the subject.

Colin wasn't sure whether he should ask, but finally his curiosity got the better of him. "Someone in your family?"

Dash sighed. "My uncle Rudy. He's dad's younger brother and has…problems. Dad's tried everything but it doesn't seem to work." He went quiet and Colin respected the silence, taking another drag of his cigarette.

"It's tough seeing someone you love go downhill, you know?" Dash said sadly. "It's a fucking shame seeing someone you love lose themselves in booze."

They both sat there for a minute in companionable silence. Then Dash spoke musingly. "You know, I've never kissed a bloke who smoked before."

Colin inhaled too much of his ciggie and choked back a cough. He ended up with Dash slapping him on the back as Colin attempted to gain his breath.

"I've never left a bloke this breathless before," Dash joked, with a sunny smile. "You okay, Tiger?"

Tiger? Colin wasn't sure where that nickname came from. He…rather liked it. He managed to take a breath and wiped his streaming eyes with the corner of the blanket he still wore like a shroud around his shoulders.

"Yeah," he hawked out. "M'good." What the hell? Did he say he wanted to kiss me?

"Tiger because of those tiger undies you wear, by the way," Dash murmured. "In case you were wondering. My personal favourite in your wardrobe."

Oh God, those would be the sexy tiger print tight briefs Colin wore for special occasions. The last time he recalled donning those was for a boy's night out with his bestie, Craig, some weeks ago. They'd gone to a new club in Cambridge, Colin flashing his fake ID to get in—Craig was eighteen already—thinking they might both meet "the one" there who would wow them over. Alas, it hadn't meant to be. They had got rather merry and—oh shit. Colin vaguely remembered hanging onto his balcony for dear life when he'd got home, trying to say hello to Dash and inviting him over for a *shimmy*. He'd done some rather weird stuff with his hips if he recalled. The rest of the evening was a blank.

"I was about to rush over and save you, 'cos you looked rather the worse for the wear and I thought you might fall off the edge," Dashiell offered. "Then you headed off inside and I thought you'd gone to bed. You weren't at the bottom of the garden so I figured you were safe." He nudged Colin, who was studying the ground wishing it would swallow him up. "And FYI? I'll shimmy with you anytime."

"I need to research Outer Mongolia and Alaska when I get home," Colin nodded sadly to himself. "I'm sure they need AI scientists out there."

Dash looked at him strangely. "What's that all about? Alaska?" he shivered. "You couldn't pay me to live there. Too bloody cold, all that snow, polar bears eating your face off…."

Colin put on a brave face. "Never mind. It's all good. You won't have to worry about me making a fool of myself anymore because I'll be...umph." His self-pity was abruptly cut off by warm fingers turning his face, and then Dash's lips claiming his in a soft kiss, sending Colin to outer space, let alone Alaska. Dash's lips stayed pressed against his as long as it took Colin to realise the gorgeous boy next door was kissing him, and after that realisation, it was all Colin could do not to maul Dash like previously referenced polar bear.

There was only a hint of tongue against Colin's lips, and he opened his mouth slightly to allow Dash entrance. Their French kiss was over far too soon, leaving Colin bereft. He opened his eyes dazedly to see Dash staring into his.

"Wow, great kiss," Dash said huskily. "Cigarette smoke doesn't taste too bad. Then again, you'd taste amazing any way." His pupils were black, his lips wet and swollen, and Colin wondered if he had the same look of awe on his face Dash had.

"Yeah, great kiss," Colin echoed. "You taste of peppermint and coffee. You should bottle it. Guys would go crazy for it."

Dash leaned back and regarded Colin. "Yeah? We could start our own range of mouthwash or chewing gum."

They grinned at each other, and Colin's chest expanded, filled with something that warmed him from the inside and sent thrills through every nerve ending in his body.

"I've been waiting for an opportunity to ask you out," Dash said, almost bashfully. "I know we've been flirting around, but there never seemed to be a right time to do it." He laughed. "Until you fell in the lake and I saved you."

Colin opened his mouth to deny the claim, then promptly shut it. Dash had rescued him and it would be churlish to disagree. Besides, he didn't truly care about anything right now other than Dash seemed to want him. Geeky Colin Tyrone MacKenzie had his very own dream boy who wanted to ask him out.

Dash waved a hand in front of him. "Earth to Tiger, anyone home?"

Colin blinked and came back to earth. "Yes, I'm thinking quietly. I do it a lot, so you'll need to get used to it. I'm surprised you like me, is all."

Dash's eyes narrowed. "Why? Because you don't look like the guys in porn or the magazines? I'm no super hunk either, Col."

"But I'm like, tall, thin, and geeky. I don't do gym. I have this brown hair my mum is always on me to have cut—"

"Hey, enough of that," Dash said fiercely. "Let me tell you what I see." He drew back. "I see this cute guy with the most gorgeous auburn hair, which shines red when the sun hits it just so. I see someone who's funny and easy to talk to. He's also one of the smartest people I know. I mean, I heard about that robot you made last year in secondary school. It was wicked. You came first in the Science-Athon Awards for building that epic bot that could pick things up and place them around a room." Dash reached up and brushed a lock of unruly hair from Colin's forehead. "And I see a sweet guy who respects his folks and has time to help his mum out wearing a bunny costume I'm sure he didn't want to. Don't you dare downplay yourself."

Wow, Dash knew all that about him? Colin didn't know whether to be proud or scared. "Well, maybe I'm not that bad," he acknowledged with a chuckle. "I love how you see me."

"Did I also mention this guy has a hot bod and is a great kisser? Because that should be taken into account too." Dash sealed that statement with another toe-curling kiss, a little more forceful this time. Any more of this and Colin would self-ignite. The sock under his pillow would be getting a really good work out tonight.

"Ow, fuck." Colin dropped the cigarette he was still holding and it fell into ash onto the ground. "Bloody hell, that hurt."

"Gives another meaning to the phrase 'burning with passion,' yeah?" Dash smirked.

Colin rubbed his burnt finger. "You think you're so clever." He drew in a breath. "Sooo. What university are you going to in September? I remember you saying you had a bit of a gap year, then you were starting. You're eighteen now, right?"

Dash nodded. "East Anglia. I'm nineteen in November. Scorpio, me." He waggled his brows. "What about you?"

"Oh, I'm doing a BSc in Artificial Intelligence at Anglia Ruskin. I'm seventeen, eighteen in September. I'm a Virgo. Not that I believe in all that stuff." He snorted.

Dash sat up, startled his eyes wide. "Oh, you don't? My mum does people's birth charts and they're fascinating. It's incredible how true some of the stuff she comes up with." He warmed to his subject. "See, I'm so like my sign. I'm a Water sign and I love water. I'm passionate, sensual," he grinned, "which bodes well for my sex life one day, and I love teasing people." He frowned. "On the downside, I can be jealous, and I like always being right."

"Hmm." Colin wrinkled his nose. "I can see all of that." He chose to ignore having learned something about Dash's sex life, which made his mind and body do things that weren't suitable in public. "So what do they say about Virgos then?" Despite his scientific brain, Colin was intrigued. He supposed reading the planets and stars was a little science-like.

"Well, Virgo's are an Earth sign, so these people are grounded. They're analytical, which is you to a tee, and hardworking." Dash warmed to his subject. "They can also be shy and over critical of themselves. They tend to like organisation, and chaos—like the stuff I cause," Dash winked "is not something they're fond of."

Colin was impressed. "Sounds about right. I'll call you Chaos from now on, seeing as how you have a name for me."

"Aww, look at us. We haven't even been dating long and we already have nicknames for each other. Tiger and Chaos. I love it."

Colin cleared his throat. "Dating?" *How the hell did I get from sizzling kisses to having a boyfriend?* Not that he was complaining, but it had all happened rather suddenly.

Dash laughed loudly. "Did I forget to tell you Scorpios are assertive and like making decisions?" The words were said with confidence, but Colin saw the slight trace of nervousness in Dash's eyes. He wasn't as self-assured on this topic as he wanted to be. "Scorpios don't kiss just anyone, you know. There has to be, you know, like a real attraction there."

Colin grinned slowly, the vulnerability of his boy-next-door appealing. "Sounds like all I have to do is go online and print off some sheet with all Scorpio characteristics and I'll know everything I need to know about you," he teased. "That makes a relationship easy, don't you think?" He frowned. "But that would be boring. I don't want to know someone that well at the start. I like to make my own impressions of people." He reached out a hand and ran a finger down Dash's cheek. "So don't make it too easy for me." The sense of control he got from seeing Dash's tongue snake out and lick his lips nervously was empowering.

Dash swallowed. "Uhm, okay. I'll leave you something to work with." His eyes focused on Colin's lips, and he swallowed again.

"You want to date me? Like, being a boyfriend and everything that goes with it?" Colin pretended to think about it. He liked making this usually-in-charge guy squirm. "I think I can live with that."

Dash growled and reached over for him. "You wanker. I thought you were going to say no for a minute." His lips covered Colin's again, and for a while, nothing entered Colin's mind but the feel of Dash's warm body against his, and the soft whispering of the plants around them as they blew in the light breeze that had come from nowhere.

When they'd finished their face-sucking, Colin leaned against Dash's shoulder, satiated and... shivering. The light breeze had turned into something colder and Colin was still damp from his lake excursion.

Dash noticed. "Oops. We've been too long making-out. You need to get dry. How could I have forgotten that?" He tucked the damp blanket solicitously around Colin's shuddering shoulders. "Come on. Let's do this."

He retrieved his bike and they began the five-minute walk to Colin's house. His teeth were chattering feverishly, and the cold bite of the wind worked its way into every muscle and bit of bare skin it could find. The weather had turned, and the bright, sunny April day was gone, giving way to ominous grey clouds and the first pitter-patter of rain.

"Shit," Colin swore as they began to run. "What is it with me and getting wet today? This sucks."

Dash gestured ahead, raindrops sparkling on his long black lashes, and dripping off his tanned skin. "Only a couple of minutes, Tiger, and we'll be home. Come on—race you." He sped across the street with his bike, grinning fiercely as someone blew their horn.

Colin sped after him, his long legs eating up the distance. He held the blanket out behind him like a cloak. "Look out, people, crazy scientist alert. Oops, sorry, Mrs Payne. Didn't mean to splash you. Jethro, you stupid dog, get out of my way!"

When he finally reached the gate to his front yard, both he and Dash were laughing crazily at their mad dash for cover.

"That was fun," Colin spluttered as he opened the gate. "Come on in, Chaos, we both need a hot drink after this. Leave your bike in the front garden, it'll be safe there."

He threw open to door to his home and squelched in, tossing his backpack into the small laundry room alongside the entrance. "Mum, I'm home. I brought a guest."

His mother Linda appeared from the downstairs bathroom. She held a handful of towels in her arms. They smelled warm and fragrant and Colin thought she'd removed them moments ago from the tumble dryer. His mum loved fresh towels in the bathroom. It was a thing of hers.

"Hello, lads. Colin, go upstairs and get changed. You're soaked. Bring something down for Dashiell as well. I'm sure you'll have something to fit him. Lovely to see you, by the way, young man. What's my Colin been getting up to?" She laid the towels down on the dining room table. "I heard the daft bugger fell in the lake and had to be rescued." She snorted loudly. "Only my Col could do something like that."

"Oi, Mum, steady on," Colin yelled as he dashed up the stairs. "It was that blasted Motability scooter. Those things are a menace." He vaguely heard his mother mumble something and then Colin was in his bedroom, dropping damp, cold clothing and drying himself off with a towel he kept on the back of his door. He scrubbed at his hair, then padded over to the chest of drawers and took out a warm, well-worn pair of sweat pants and a long-sleeved tee-shirt with the slogan "All those moments will be lost in time, like tears in rain." *Bladerunner*—the original of course—was Colin's all-time favourite film. He'd jerked off to Rutger Hauer's white hair and startling blue eyes many times. The man was a legend.

He rummaged around and found something similar he thought Dash would fit into. Clasping it to his chest with a smug thought of *Boyfriend's wearing my clothes already* he ran down the stairs. Dash stood in the kitchen as Colin's mum made tea. Colin pushed the bundle of clothing into his arms.

"Here you go. That should do. Bathroom's through there if you want to change."

Dash nodded his thanks and took his leave. Colin sat down at the kitchen island and watched his mother pour tea.

"You all right, Col? Mrs Jensen said you'd take a bit of a tumble. She said our lovely lad from next door helped you out." She sat down next to him and pushed a mug of tea over to him.

Colin nodded. "Yeah, he did. We, err, went to the allotment, and had a chat before it started pissing with rain. He's a good sort."

She nodded her head with a small smile. "Uh-huh. Not hard on the eyes, either is he?"

"Mum," Colin said, pretending to be scandalised. "While I agree, let's not objectify the poor man."

She rolled her eyes. "Oh heaven forbid, let's not." They shared a secret smile. Colin's coming out to his folks had been easy enough. He'd done it when he was fourteen and certain the tingles he got in his nether regions when he saw certain guys, coupled with the fact he jacked off to several male teen idols was proof enough girls didn't do it for him. His mum and dad had listened, hugged him, told him they'd support him and continued watching "The Sweeney" without any further ado.

Colin wondered what Dashiell's experience had been like with his family. No doubt now they were dating, he'd hear soon enough.

"Where's Dad? I thought he'd be here." Colin's dad owned the small hardware store in town—his pride and joy—but Colin didn't think he'd be working on Easter Sunday. He thought there might be rules around that sort of thing.

"Your dad went to fetch Louie at the station. He's coming round for dinner tonight."

Louie was Dad's best friend who lived in London. Colin liked the man even if he was a bit of a poser because he was a big wig in some financial company in the city.

Dash came back into the kitchen clad in Colin's best tracksuit, a navy-blue French Connection one that seemed a little long in the legs but otherwise fit well.

"That's better," he announced as he sat down on a kitchen stool. Colin's mum pushed a cup of tea his way. "Thank you, Mrs MacKenzie. That's lovely."

"Call me Linda, love. I have a feeling we'll be seeing a bit of each other." His mother stood up and picked up her tea. "I'll love and leave you boys. I've got some "Line of Duty" episodes to catch up on." She waved a hand and left.

Colin looked at Dash and they grinned at each other.

"So…" Dash drawled. He fidgeted with the string tie around his trouser waistband.

"So indeed….." Colin drawled back.

"We good?" Dash asked, his face uncertain. "I mean, we're going to do this, yeah? Go out?"

Colin nodded. "I'm on board. I mean, we're both going to university in September too so we'll be busy then, but at least we don't live far from each other." He frowned. "I never asked you what you were studying?"

"An MA in Agriculture and Rural Studies. I want to do something related to the environment, helping under-privileged countries, stuff like that. I'm hoping it'll take me abroad a bit. I'd love to travel."

Hopefully not *too* soon, Colin thought with a pang. Let's get to know each other a bit more first. "That sounds cool. I know you're interested in that sort of thing." He cleared his throat. "So, I think we should do this properly. Friday night we should have a date night. A film, some dinner and a drink, and see what happens. You game?"

Dashiell stood up and gave Colin a bright grin. "I think that sounds like fun. Not that today wasn't, but another thing you should know about Scorpios. We're ro-man-tic." He drew out the word.

Colin chuckled. "Then it's a date. I look forward to it." He stood up too. "I'd best get upstairs, have a shower before dinner. Thanks for a great day even if it did start out rather unpleasant."

"You're welcome." Dash pressed a soft kiss against Colin's cheek. "I've got your number. Text you later after dinner?"

"Sure." Colin was down for some sexting if that's what Dash meant.

"Cool. Well then, I'd be better be off." Dash ran a hand through Clin's unruly damp hair. "See ya, Tiger."

With a flash of white teeth, Dash left and Colin sat there daydreaming until his tea was cold and his mother told him to get a move on. He couldn't help but float up the stairs to the bathroom.

I'm dating. OMG. I'm going to have to tell my folks. Although I think Mum knows already.

This year, the Easter Bunny had outdone himself.

He'd brought Colin a boyfriend.

HOMECOMING

Emily Mims

Chapter One

Clay parked his ancient pickup truck behind the Durango Street Theatre, stepped into waves of August heat shimmering off the parking lot asphalt, and wiped his sweaty palms on his jeans. It was ridiculous to be nervous. Everyone had been warm and welcoming when he'd been here last week to register for Academy classes. The director had gone out of her way to make him feel at home and had clapped her hands when he told her about his previous theater experience. "We'll put you into the advanced classes." She'd been enthusiastic. "*Oklahoma* has a lot of good male singing roles, and we'd love to have you be one of them."

So would he.

Still, he was the newbie and would have to prove himself. He snaked his way through the back of the theater and after a couple of wrong turns found the empty rehearsal room for the advanced singing class. He plopped down into one of the circle of chairs and checked his phone, grimacing when he realized he was almost a half hour early. He settled in for the wait and went online to check his emails and social media. Most were crap he deleted, but the fourth one down from little sister Amanda caught his eye.

I miss you, big brother. Singapore sucks. Wish I could have stayed behind with you.

Wish you could, too. But give it a chance. It might be okay.

Not that Amanda had been given the choice he had. "Clay, you can come with us and finish high school at the American school in Singapore, or you can live with your father in San Antonio and finish there," his mother said when he'd protested the move. "I've already talked to Bear and he'd be willing to take you in if that's what you want."

San Antonio versus Singapore. No brainer if there ever was one.

So here he was, his senior year in a new high school, and taking classes at the Durango Street Theatre Academy. It'd been his father who'd suggested it. "Your mom said you were into singing and acting, and one of my Army buddies has his daughter there. His girl loves it, and he thought you might too." He'd been surprised at the recommendation. If ever there was a pair of buzz-cut butch middle-aged men, it was Jake Pierce and Angus "Bear" Bustamante. Gun racks on their oversized pickups. Need he say more?

Actually, he didn't know his father all that well. His folks had divorced when he was a toddler, and what he knew about his father came from occasional activity-filled weekends between deployments. His mother had never bad-mouthed his dad, but from her occasional comments he'd figured his dad was more into being an Army Ranger than a family man. The articles in *Army Times*, the salad bar on his dress uniform, and the admiration and respect his fellow soldiers showed him pretty much told the story. His father was a fierce warrior and hero. A man no son could ever live up to, no matter how hard he tried.

Especially his small gay son.

Which would be a disaster if Bear ever found out. No way would his colonel father be okay with having a gay child. He'd be angry and disappointed. Him knowing would be a one-way ticket to Singapore on the first available flight.

But it wasn't going to be a problem. Bear would never find out.

Slowly, boys around his age from all walks of life came into the rehearsal room. The director had said the Academy was a cross-section of the community, and she hadn't been wrong. The boys pushed, shoved, and high-fived one another, and greeted him with a head nod, or the occasional friendly smile. The female pianist and the instructor, an older man with scars on his face, had taken their places when the hottest guy Clay had ever seen darted in and sat on the other side of the room, right in Clay's sightline. *Holy hell, where have you been all my life?* The gorgeous dude kicked his backpack under his chair and fist-bumped the guy next to him.

Damn. Clay hardened just from looking at the guy.

So not good perving on straight guy.

Their instructor introduced himself as Mr. Aldrete, and then outlined what he expected them to accomplish in the next months, including learning advanced singing techniques using the songs from *Oklahoma.* Cool, but it was hard to keep his mind on the lesson. He kept glancing at the hot guy with classic high cheekbones and a square jawline. Lucky bastard probably had a string of girls chasing him, and gay guys jackin' off thinking about him.

Mr. Aldrete demonstrated an advanced breathing technique, and then motioned for the class to stand, giving Clay a better look at the bangin', smokin', sizzlin' hot bod across the room. Tall. Broad shoulders. Narrow hips. He tried not to make it obvious, but it was difficult to keep his eyes off the dude. Determined not to embarrass himself, he turned his attention back to the instructor, hoping to hell his gawking hadn't been noticed.

But it was hard not to look. Damn, the dude had thick, curly mahogany hair. Total GQ.

Mr. Aldrete had the class practice the technique a few times. "Now we're going to practice using a couple of the songs from *Oklahoma*." He handed out song sheets and signaled to the pianist. They sang it a couple of times before Mr. Aldrete pointed to a boy two down from Clay. "Jace, let's hear you do it."

The boy did a respectable if not spectacular rendition of the first verse and chorus. Mr. Aldrete called on a couple more boys to sing and then pointed to the hot guy. "Justin, you're standing there dying to do this, aren'tcha?"

Justin.

"Sure am." Justin grinned. The pianist played the intro and Justin came in. His voice was in the tenor range, but he delivered a beautiful rendition of the song, using Mr. Aldrete's breathing technique perfectly, sustaining the notes longer than anyone else had.

Justin wasn't only hot. He sang like a dream.

Mr. Aldrete nodded with satisfaction. "Gentlemen, that's how it's done." He glanced around the room before gesturing to Clay. "I do believe you're the new student. Would you like to introduce yourself and show us what you got? Let's have you sing 'Oh What a Beautiful Morning.'"

Clay nodded and introduced himself. He sang the old favorite, using Mr. Aldrete's technique to control his air flow. It didn't hurt he'd performed *Oklahoma* last year at his old high school, or that his baritone was much bigger than his five-seven frame conveyed. He belted out the song for all it was worth and was treated to a round of whistles and cheers when he'd finished. "Damn, dude, talk about rockin' it," Justin said. "That was awesome." Then he winked at Clay in front of the entire class.

Clay felt the heat rise in his face. *Shit. Justin must've noticed Clay checking him out.* He glanced around, prepared to see knowing grins and smirks, but saw only appreciation for his performance. Either they hadn't noticed the wink or they didn't care. Big question—Was Justin gay, or was he acknowledging Clay's admiration.

Mr. Aldrete asked Clay a couple of questions about his previous experience, and the class moved on. He glanced across the room, and damn if Justin wasn't checking him out. Subtly, of course. This wasn't LA or New York. He wasn't going to be out here even in an accepting environment like the theater.

Damn, he hoped Justin liked what he saw.

They practiced their breathing for a few more minutes and spent the rest of the session on songs from *Oklahoma*. "Jessica told me the production will be double cast, and there are six singing parts for males as well as places in the ensemble," Mr. Aldrete said. "If you want a singing part, you have a good chance of getting it. But nothing's guaranteed, so go home and practice. Don't everybody try out for Will or Curly. The featured spots have a wealth of possibility."

"I remember," Justin piped up. "You did Jud Fry. Without the makeup. You rocked it, Mr. A."

The instructor's cheeks turned a little red. "Thanks. Always good to hear. Okay, guys. See you next week."

The boys scattered. Clay had only one class on Tuesdays and was free to go. Not that he was in a big hurry to go home. His father had left this morning for a week of temporary duty and Clay had a stack of TV dinners and strict instructions to behave. "I'm not happy leaving you alone, but your mom assures me you're one hundred percent trustworthy. But still. No entertaining and keep the place presentable. If you get lonesome, Jake's lady friend cooks up a mean plate of fried chicken, and they said they'd love to have you over." Clay wouldn't bother Jake, and figured he'd heat up a couple of the TV dinners, make himself a sandwich, or pick up a sack of tacos on the way home.

He was almost to his truck when he heard a sharp whistle behind him and whipped around. Justin, with his longs legs and swiveling hips, was coming across the parking lot. "Yo, new boy. Slow down."

Clay slowed, but still reached his truck before Justin caught up with him. They leaned against the fender side by side. "I'm Justin Hardin. You're Clay." Clay nodded. He was too tongue-tied to say anything, and waited for Justin to break the silence. "So, you new to town or just the Durango?" Justin asked.

"Town. I moved here last week from Chicago. My stepfather got transferred to Singapore and I didn't want to go. My mom sent me to finish my senior year here with my dad."

Justin's grin brought out two incredible dimples. "Do I offer congrats or condolences?"

"I'd rather be here than Singapore. Otherwise, jury's still out."

"Gotcha. Say, wanna grab a burger, or is your dad slaving at home over the stove?"

As if. "He's TDY this week. A burger sounds good."

"Okay, then. There's a good place about a mile north on the street out front." He motioned with his thumb. "Meet you there."

Justin hopped in a Prius and motioned for Clay to follow. Clay's heart pounded and his palms were slick with sweat as he gripped the steering wheel. Christ. Standing beside the guy gave Clay a major hard-on. Yeah, he was fuckin' gorgeous, but Justin also intrigued him. Clay wanted to get to know him better. If Justin was straight, he'd be good to have as a friend. But it'd be so much better if he was gay.

Before Clay started to fantasize, he knew if he started anything with Justin, his father was going to figure out real damn quick his one and only son was not gonna follow in daddy's footsteps. Which was the absolute last thing he wanted to happen.

Shit.

Chapter Two

Clay was the cutest damn dude Justin had ever seen. Curly dark hair, snapping golden brown eyes, pouty lips, a bangin' bod, and fantastic baritone. Hotness personified.

Justin was getting hard looking at him.

Clay stared across the table at Justin's burger. "What in the world is a tostada burger?"

"Meat, refried beans, cheese, crushed chips and salsa. Best burger ever. No tostada burgers in Chicago?"

"No, but Chicago hot dogs have the ones here beat hands down."

"No doubt." Justin looked across the table. "Okay. We know I grew up here, you grew up in Chicago, our moms are divorced and remarried, we both have a sister, we're seniors, but in different high schools, we both love acting, singing, and burgers. Anything else we should cover?"

Clay blushed and looked down.

Yeah, I'm so gonna ask. "Gay or straight?"

Clay looked up, surprised. "Ah, gay. You?"

"Oh, yeah."

Clay looked relieved. "Good. I don't wanna be crushing on a guy who's lusting after the ladies."

"Nope. Ladies are fine. Lovely. But they don't ring my bell. Your family okay with it?"

Clay's eyes went wide. "My family doesn't know. My mom might, or she at least suspects. My father doesn't, and if I have my way, he never will."

"Why not?" Justin asked. "You ashamed of who you are?"

"Fuck no. But he's not type of person who'd be all open-minded. Your folks?"

"I haven't come out and told them, but I've been me, and they're take me as I am types. College professors with liberal leanings. Mom's talking about running for the City Council, as an independent, of course. I figure, when I bring home my first boyfriend, they'll be all whatever, and have you had dinner yet."

"Must be nice to have that kind of freedom. I don't."

"Why? Your dad a homophobe or something?"

"Or something. He's a colonel in the Army. A ranger, and every cliché that goes with it. Be damned if I want him to know."

"So what are you gonna do? Hide in the closet all your life? You need to have the courage to be who you are."

"Yo," Clay snapped. "My dad's a genuine, bona-fide war hero. I look up to him. He loves me, and I'll be damned if I disappoint him." He turned his attention to his meal.

Damn. Not cool. The last thing he'd meant to do was piss Clay off.

They ate in silence for a couple of minutes, and then Justin changed the subject and asked Clay about the productions he'd done in Chicago. They paid and walked out to their vehicles.

It'd gotten dark while they were inside, and the parking lot was lit by the glow of the business signs lining the street. They stared at one another in the muted light, Justin's heart pounding as he grew hard at what he saw Clay's eyes.

They moved toward one another and stopped mere inches apart. They were so close he could hear Clay breathing. "I gotta kiss you," he said as he reached out and yanked Clay close, covering his lips.

Clay stiffened for a moment, then relaxed into the embrace. Touching, tasting, exploring, they held each other, and as their hands roamed, Justin moved his fingers up Clay's muscular back and down to his hard butt. His cock swelled, and he could feel Clay's hard length against his thigh. He kissed and nipped until Clay opened his mouth, and then their tongues tangled awkwardly. Their lack of experience showed, but Justin didn't care, and from Clay's enthusiasm it didn't seem to matter to him either. They stood kissing for long moments, plastered together from head to toe.

When Justin raised his head, he was breathing hard and his cock was throbbing. "Holy shit, Is it always like that with you?"

"I-I-I-no. God, I wish it was."

Justin held Clay by the shoulders and gazed into his eyes. "It's us. You and me. The combination." Clay nodded. "I want to go out with you next weekend. Have some fun and kiss you some more."

Clay didn't answer, and Justin felt himself start to wilt. "Or was what we did a one-off?"

"Hell, no." He could see Clay swallow. "This city's big, right? Big enough we can go out and not run into anybody we know."

Justin froze. "You wanna see me on the DL?"

"How else am I gonna hang with you without my dad finding out? Either we go far out of town, or I let him think we're trolling for girls."

"That sucks, and it's not cool."

"It's also the way it has to be. *Please* try to understand."

Justin hesitated. It would be easy to get in the car and drive away. But it would mean turning his back on the cutest, hottest guy to come his way in forever. "All right. Next Saturday night. I'll meet you in front of Subway at La Cantera. It's about twenty miles from here. We'll eat and if there're no good movies showing, we can go to the arcade behind the movie theater. Is that far enough away from your dad's stomping ground to suit you?"

Clay nodded. "We should be okay. Here. Give me your contact info."

They swapped phones and entered their information. Justin wanted to kiss Clay, but he needed to sort his head. He gave him a peck on the cheek, then sat behind the wheel and waited until Clay pulled out of the parking lot before starting his car.

The secrecy pissed him off big time, but he'd put up with it for now. Maybe Clay was justified. He didn't know. He didn't have a father like that.

What he did know—it wasn't going to fly forever. If they kept on seeing each other, Clay was going to have to be honest and come out.

Justin wasn't going to be anyone's dirty little secret.

Chapter Three

Welcome AC blasted Clay as he shut the back door to the Durango Street Theatre. Damn, September in San Antonio was every bit as hot as summer. He'd said something to that effect this morning and Bear chuckled. "Kid, it's hot here until November and never really gets cold, not like you're used to. You may as well put on your swimsuit and go back to the pool."

Or come to the nice air-conditioned Academy and sing. He made his way through the now familiar rabbit warren to the backstage restroom for a pit stop. He was coming out when he spotted a familiar face and cheeky grin. Immediately, he got hard. Same as when he caught a whiff of Justin's aftershave in his truck after a make out session. Or when he thought about Justin while he was supposed to be studying for an English lit test. Or anytime Justin so much as crossed his mind.

He spent a lot of time hard these days.

Justin glanced around. "Coast is clear," he said as he yanked Clay into the men's dressing room and shut the door. He wrapped Clay in his arms and laid a hard, sweet kiss on him. "Sorry, I couldn't wait," he said as he opened the door a crack and peered out. "Come on before somebody spots us. What with you wanting to keep us secret." Justin sounded pissed off.

Over the last couple of weeks, the topic of Clay's deep closet life had led to more than a few arguments. Clay pled, Justin relented, and they went out miles away from San Antonio.

They liked the same things, had loads of fun together, and in a short time, had come to care about one another. But Justin never let up about wanting to be out. He wanted the world to know he and Clay were dating, and didn't understand Clay's reluctance to stand up to his father. "It's not like you've told your mother," Clay had said when Justin last brought it up.

"Maybe not. But she knows I'm going out with you, and she know it's not to pick up chicks."

The argument wasn't going away any time soon.

They sat down next to each other as the room filled. Mr. Aldrete had brought a tall dude who was seriously hot. Justin leaned over. "That's Mr. A's husband Wade. Mr. A's one lucky SOB."

Husband? The gorgeous young man was married to Mr. A? Oh, yeah. Mr. A was a lucky SOB.

Mr. A introduced Wade to the class without saying *this is my husband*, but their matching wedding rings and their obvious affection was evident. Wade sang, and had one of the clearest, sweetest tenors Clay'd ever heard. Even better than Justin's, which was saying something. He burned with curiosity. More than once Mr. A had mentioned his children. Yet he was married to a man. He wondered how Mr. A managed it. How he and Wade handled being so *out*.

Wade was an awesome teacher, and the class ended too soon. The rest of the boys scattered, but Clay hung back. "What are you doing?" Justin asked. "I thought we'd go out for burgers."

"We will. But I want to talk to Mr. A. Meet you in the parking lot."

Clay hoped Justin would take the hint, but he didn't move. Clay waited until the room was empty of students, and the pianist left before approaching the two men. Wade broke into a big smile. "So you're the new guy with the awesome baritone. Owen's bragged on you more than once." He turned to Justin and asked, "How's it goin'?"

"Fantastic," Justin said, then nudged Clay. "Ask away."

Clay felt his face redden and he fought the urge to run. Finding his balls, he asked, "I was kinda wondering. I have a friend who's gay, and I-he doesn't know how to manage it. Being gay, I mean. How you do it? With kids and a husband, you know? And everybody knowing?" His face burned and he wanted to fall into the crack in the floor.

The men looked at one another and a silent message passed between them. "I live my life one day at a time like anybody does. Work my job. Pay my bills. Spend time with my family. Is that what you're asking?"

"Or does your friend want to know how we manage being gay and everyone knowing it?" Wade asked. Clay nodded. "To be honest, it wasn't easy at first. I didn't want anyone to know. I didn't want to disappoint my mom."

Sounds familiar.

Wade continued. "But my man here wanted the world to know, and he convinced me it was better to be honest about who I am. A few folks weren't happy, but most everyone who really cares about me is fine with it."

"So it's better to be honest," Justin said with satisfaction.

Owen looked from Justin to Clay. "If you can be," he said. "Wade and I were both adults when we came out. Big difference in coming out as an adult and coming out as a teenager. Especially if you live with adults who aren't on board."

"So sometimes it's better not to tell," Clay said thoughtfully.

"Sometimes. It all depends on the situation," Wade said. "I recommend judicious honesty. Honesty if and when you can be. Discretion when you can't. And patience. You won't be teenagers much longer, and as adults you'll have freedoms you don't enjoy at this point in your life. Or your friend's life."

Wade's eyes danced. He knew damned well there was no *friend*.

Clay nodded. "Thanks. Both of you."

"Any time," they said in unison.

The boys were silent until they reached the parking lot. Then Justin elbowed Clay in the ribs. "See. I told you. Honesty's the best policy."

"That is not what they said," Clay muttered.

Justin shrugged. "That's what I heard."

"They said judicious honesty. Which means you tell only if you can. If you can't, you keep your mouth shut." He turned around and yanked open his truck door. "I'm hungry. We can talk after we eat."

They met at the burger place where they'd become regulars. Clay thought the argument had cost him his appetite, but he still managed to kill a double meat tostada burger and a basket of fries. Justin finished the same and then demolished an old-fashioned milkshake. They paid for dinner and walked to their parked cars behind the café. Justin leaned against Clay's truck and crossed his arms in front of him. "Now are you ready to talk?"

"Do we have to?" Clay asked. "You want me to come out. You think I should be 'who I am.'" He made air quotes with his fingers. "You don't give a damn what the consequences might be."

"What's the worst that could happen?"

"I could get sent to fucking Singapore if Dad decides he doesn't want a gay kid in his house."

"He's not gonna do that. You said he loves you. He's gonna love you, gay or straight."

"Yeah, but maybe he won't be as proud." He sighed. "Why in hell is it so important for me to come out? What's wrong with what we're doing now?"

"Homecoming."

"What does Homecoming have to do with it?"

"Clay, don't be stupid. I want to take you to Homecoming. As my date."

"Oh. *Oh.*"

"Yeah. It's a big deal at my school. Corsages and boutonnieres. The big game. A semiformal dance. Dinner at a fancy restaurant. I want to go, and I want you to go with me. You can't do that if you're not out."

"I don't know. I want to. God, I want to so bad. I don't know what to say."

"Maybe this will help you make up your mind." Justin turned to Clay and drew him into his arms. They'd taken to parking in the back under the cover of darkness, away from prying eyes.

They were alone except for a stray cat scuttling under the car. Clay melted into Justin's arms and opened his lips. The boys had kissed many times in the last month, their embraces feverish with intensity. Tonight was no exception.

Clay's heart pounded as Justin's hands roamed his body, cupping his butt and pulling him close. Their hard-ons swelled, throbbing against each other.

Clay stroked Justin's back and shoulders, his fingers sweeping over the hard, muscular landscape he'd memorized. A landscape he wished he could touch without the t-shirt between them. More than once they'd talked about parking someplace private and *going all the way*, but neither of them was ready to take that step. But they kissed and touched and caressed the hell out of each other.

They clung together for long moments, their lips and tongues fighting a sensual duel. When Justin raised his head, he asked with a wicked grin, "Any closer to making up your mind?"

Clay blinked and shook his head. Talk about a bucket of cold water. "Not-not really," he stammered as he stepped back.

Justin's grin disappeared. "What's it gonna take? At some point you've gotta be who you are." His voice softened and he reached for Clay's hand. "I'm not trying to be an asshole. I really care about you, and I worry. Hiding who you are can't be good. Not in the long run."

"You think I don't know?" Clay said, not trying to hide his anguish. "I care about you too. If it weren't for my father, I'd stand up on the roof of the damned theater and shout it to the world. But I care about him, and I don't want to make him angry. Disappointed. I sure don't want to hurt him."

"So is that a *no*?" Justin asked quietly. Clay cringed inwardly at the look on Justin's face. He'd hurt him, but he couldn't bring himself to say yes.

He took a deep breath. "I'll think about it. That's the best I can do."

"Okay." Justin held out his arms. "One for the road. Then I gotta get home."

Clay moved into his arms. This kiss was tender and sweet. He wished with all his heart he could be the boyfriend Justin deserved. Slowly they drew apart and stepped back. "I'll think about it," Clay promised.

"Please," Justin whispered.

***

The lights were on and his dad's pickup was in the garage when Clay pulled into the driveway. He found his father dumping a duffel of dirty clothes into the washing machine. "You're home early," Clay said as Bear threw a couple of laundry pods in the washer. "How was Jump School?"

"Same old, same old. Twentysomethings all hot to jump out of perfectly good airplanes." Bear's eyes danced. "It was fun. It's always fun."

"Did a little jumping yourself, didn't you?"

"Of course. Somebody has to show them how." He set the washer on heavy duty. "I take it from the onions on your breath you've already had dinner. Come keep me company while I eat mine. Or eat a little more. I got enough tacos for the two of us."

"Cool."

He followed his dad into the kitchen, where a big sack with a grease spot sat in the middle of the kitchen table. Clay got out paper plates and napkins while Bear opened sodas. They sat across from one another and his father ripped open the sack. "So how was school this week?" he asked as he gestured at the bag.

Clay found two *carne guisada* and moved them to his plate. Bear fished out four *al pastor*. "English and history are easy peasy. I'm scrambling a little in trig. My math teachers for the last two years sucked."

"The perils of public school. How about the Durango?"

Clay lit up. "I got the part I wanted."

"Good for you. What part?"

"Jud Fry."

"You want to play the bad guy?"

"I played Curly last year. Wanted to try something new."

"Makes sense. So tell me about it."

Clay told him how *Oklahoma* was shaping up and Bear told him about Jump School. Eventually they got too serious about the tacos to talk. Clay studied the increasingly familiar face across the table. He looked nothing like his blunt-featured, craggy-faced father.

Bear topped six feet and Clay guessed no one had said he was handsome. If it weren't for their identical golden-brown eyes and curly hair, Clay would've wondered if Bear was really his father.

They didn't share the same interests. Bear was all about hunting and fishing and martial arts, and he was tone deaf. But he always asked about the stuff Clay was into and his pride in Clay's theatrical accomplishments wasn't forced. Bear would be at the Durango on opening night with a big smile on his face and a "That's my boy" on his lips. But when news segments about gay and trans people in the military were on, Bear would scowl and say murmur things like, "This is such bullshit."

Justin couldn't understand.

A son didn't disappoint a man like Bear.

***

Justin pulled up in front of the house and parked on the street. His mother's fundraiser must've ended early. She'd said something about a meeting afterwards, and that must be what all the cars in the driveway were about. The front door was unlocked and he slipped inside. His older sister Mindy's bedroom door was shut and he heard voices coming from the family room. Some of the voices were familiar. Curious, he ran up the stairs and peered down from the darkened loft. He recognized precinct chairman Diego Vargas and vice-chair Stephanie Krause and a couple more people, but many of the faces were unfamiliar. His mother, Delores, was sitting in her usual easy chair and his stepfather, Russell, was serving drinks.

Justin was about to retreat to his room when Diego said. "I really think you have a shot at it, Delores. You could win the election."

"She'd make a great city councilwoman, wouldn't she?" Russell asked sounding all proud.

"You're kind," Mom said. "Especially you, Russell. But I doubt I could win."

There was a chorus of *sure you coulds* "Delores, you check off all the boxes," Diego went on. "Female, Latina, but married to an Anglo. Highly educated, and visibly active in the political community: a volunteer at your church and at the schools. Your kids are old enough to fend for themselves, and your job gives you the flexibility to attend meetings and a lot of daytime events. You'd be a great candidate." He looked around the room. "Am I not correct?"

A man Justin didn't recognize gestured with his drink. "Pretty much, but I see a problem. Delores is a known liberal with progressive views. Some would say too much."

"Not a problem," Russell countered. "Delores can soft-pedal our views. We don't have to be so publicly liberal."

"Not a bad idea," Diego said thoughtfully to a chorus of *'that's right'*.

Justin froze. If his mom was soft-pedaling her liberalism, how was his coming out going to go over? She might not be too enamored at having an openly gay son.

"Wait a minute." His mother stood and the room went quiet. "I haven't said I'll do it, and you're already telling me what I can and can't say as a candidate. Sure, I've always wanted to run for office, but I never wanted it badly enough to compromise my beliefs, and I don't want it that badly now. If I agree to run, I have to be true to myself. I won't abandon my causes or soft-pedal my liberal convictions."

"She's right," Stephanie said. "I'm in."

"Absolutely," Diego said a little too quickly.

Everyone seemed to be on board with Delores' pronouncement, except Russell who protested a couple of times. Justin wasn't surprised. Russell was an asshole. Always had been, always would be.

At least he was a liberal asshole.

Justin breathed a sigh of relief. It wasn't going to be a problem. He'd talk with her and Russell soon. Then he'd get Clay to say *yes*.

He smiled.

Homecoming was going to be so much fun.

Chapter Four

With a sense of foreboding, Clay parked his car behind the burger café and sat for a few minutes watching the rain hit the windshield. The skies had opened about an hour ago, dumping a torrent of cooling October rain on a parched and dusty city, drenching pathetic looking yards and running in huge rivers down low-lying streets. Bear had called him from the base. "Do *not* drive into any low-water crossings, whatever you do. This town's known for flash floods and even a foot and a half of water can sweep a car away."

Clay had promised he'd be careful. He tried to call off dinner, but Justin was insistent. "We need to talk about it," he'd snapped when Clay tried to beg off. "Homecoming. Either over burgers or on your dad's front porch. I don't give a shit which."

Justin was tired of Clay putting him off, and Clay didn't blame him. Justin needed to buy tickets to the game and the dance. They needed to order boutonnieres, make reservations, buy clothes.

Clay crossed his arms on the steering wheel and laid his head against it. He still didn't know what to do. He and Justin had grown close in the three weeks since Homecoming came up. They'd gone out every weekend to movies and the arcade. They'd eaten countless burgers and tacos at some of the city's best holes-in-the-wall.

Justin introduced Clay to the Riverwalk. Once, they'd bought a six pack at a sleazy stop and rob and gotten buzzed. They'd kissed, touched, and caressed one another to the point Clay had gone off in his jeans. They hadn't used the "L" word, but Clay was feeling it and he thought Justin was too. He wanted to go to Homecoming with Justin so bad he could taste it.

Surprisingly, Clay was starting to love his big, gruff bear of a father, and the last thing he wanted was to disappoint him.

Justin pulled up beside him and got out, getting drenched in the process. Clay went to get out of the truck but Justin yanked open the passenger door and slipped inside, dripping water all over the seat. "I thought we were eating," Clay said.

Justin shook the water out of his hair. "I see no reason to ruin a good meal with a fight. So hit me. Are you coming with me to Homecoming?"

"Justin, I—"

"Cut the crap, Clay. Yes or no."

"Jesus, why are you acting like this? You know why I'm hesitant. Or is not wanting to hurt my dad too hard to comprehend?"

"How about not wanting to hurt me?" Justin asked quietly. "I've had it with sneaking around. If you don't care enough about me to go as my date to Homecoming then you don't care enough about me to be my boyfriend. Is that so hard for *you* to comprehend?"

Clay stiffened. "I comprehend an ultimatum real well, dude. I don't do ultimatums. They piss me off. Can you comprehend that?"

"Loud and clear. Real damn loud and clear." Justin yanked open the truck door and a moment later was roaring out of the parking lot. Clay wiped angry tears off his cheeks and started his engine.

Problem solved.

***

Justin pulled the front door shut behind him and slipped up the stairs. He was hungry, but his mother was having another planning session with the precinct bigwigs and he had no desire to wade through the middle of her meeting.

If he'd been smart, he would've gone into the burger café, or at least picked up something to eat after Academy class, but seeing Clay for the first time since they'd broken up last week had shaken him so badly he hadn't thought about food until he was already parked in front of his house.

It ripped him to shreds seeing the guy he missed so much. He'd taken a seat as far away from Clay as he could. He couldn't keep from glancing across the room, hoping Clay was sneaking looks back at him. But no. Clay was looking everywhere but at Justin. The one time he met Clay's gaze, the frost was enough to freeze his balls. He shouldn't've lost his temper and issued an ultimatum. But it hurt knowing Clay didn't think enough of him to acknowledge him publicly, and was more worried about what his macho father thought than how much his refusal made Justin feel.

He hit the top step and was about to head for his bedroom when his stepfather's words stopped him in his tracks. "Damn it, Delores. You can't come out in favor of funding a center specializing in gay adoptions. Do you want to win the election, or don't you?"

He'd never in his life heard his stepfather say the word "gay" in that tone of voice. Instead of going to his bedroom, he plopped down on the loft sofa. The immediate chorus of raised voices made it impossible to understand anything, but after a moment it died down and he heard Diego's voice. "Russell, I hate to say it, but you have a point. Delores, you don't have to come out against funding the agency. Don't comment either way. Smile enigmatically and say something generic."

"What about staying true to my beliefs?" she demanded. "I told you going in I wasn't compromising."

"Yes, you did. After the election you'll be free to speak your mind and vote your conscience. But not yet," Diego said.

"Especially not with all the military and retired military in the precinct," Russell added. "Think about who populates the Army and the Air Force. It's all flag-wavin', gun-totin' good old boys."

Like Bear Bustamante. Justin winced.

"Are the soldiers and airmen really like that?" Delores asked quietly.

"I don't know. But why take the chance they are?" Diego countered solemnly.

Justin heard enough. Maybe Clay had a point. If soldiers were prejudiced against gays to the point his mother had to take it into consideration to win an election, maybe Clay shouldn't come out to his father. He slipped to his room and sent Clay a text.

I was wrong. Sorry. Get together?

Three dots appeared almost immediately. *On my way to El Macho for tacos. Mt me there.*

Justin Googled the taco bar and found Clay waiting in the parking lot. He pulled in and got in the passenger side of Clay's truck. "I'm sorry. I was wrong and you don't have to do Homecoming if you don't want to," he said in a rush. "I've missed you." Clay stared across the truck at him. "Say something, please."

"Why?"

"Why what?"

Clay looked at him doubtfully. "Why the change of heart? Last week told me either go to Homecoming or we were through. Now you're sorry. I've missed you too, but I don't want to get back together and find myself in the exact same position I was before. Being pressured to do something I don't think I can do."

"Something I overheard tonight in Mom's planning session. They're telling her to soft-pedal her position on opening a gay adoption agency. They don't want her to alienate all the military voters. From what Russell and the precinct chairman said, prejudice against gays in the military is bad. I didn't realize what you were up against before. Now I do. I want to go with you, but I don't want to do something that's gonna get you kicked out of the house. Or worse." He reached across the bench seat and took Clay's hand. "I care about you."

Clay clasped his hand. "I care about you too. Come here and let me show you how much."

Justin slid across the wide seat and melted into Clay's arms. They held one another as their lips fused, their mouths opened, and their tongues tangled. Justin felt the blood pounding in his ears and his cock swelled, pushing insistently against the seam of his jeans.

He yanked up Clay's t-shirt up and ran his hands over his bare back, loving the feel of his skin. Clay broke the kiss and leaned back long enough to yank off Justin's shirt. "Jesus, you're sporting a lot of hair," he said admiringly as he ran his fingers up Justin's chest. "I wish."

"Why? You don't need it." He palmed Clay's bare nipple. "Gorgeous. Absolutely gorgeous."

They fell together again, chest to chest. This close, Justin felt Clay's hard-on swelling in his jeans and reached down to palm it through the taut fabric. Clay stroked Justin's back before sinking lower, caressing his waist before drifting down to fondle his denim-covered butt.

Bliss. It was bliss being back in Clay's arms, kissing and touching him without a layer of clothing covering their upper bodies. A part of him was tempted to undo his belt and free his erection, but it would be dangerous in the extreme in a public parking lot. As it was, they were going to have to put their shirts on soon.

But not yet. Not until he had touched Clay to his fill, and Clay had done the same. They explored until they were both out of breath and panting. It was Clay who finally pulled away. "Damn, I went off in my jeans again. So much for going in for a taco plate."

Justin looked down at his own cock. "I'll have a session in the shower tonight for sure. Do the drive through and we can talk in the truck."

They pulled on their shirts and put in a massive taco order. Clay pulled out his favorite *carne guisada* and handed Justin the box with his puffy tacos. He scooted to the side so they could put the food on the seat between them. Justin took a bite of taco and moaned. "Either this is rockin'or I'm really hungry. I was too upset to eat much this week."

"I didn't exactly set records myself." Clay stuffed half a *carne guisada* in his mouth. "I missed you. I almost called you to say I'd go."

"You don't have to come out on my account. I don't want you to get into trouble at home."

"I didn't realize how much I wanted to go until it was off the table." He inhaled the rest of his taco. "You think we could go anyway?"

"How are we gonna do that if you're not out?"

"I could pretend I'm taking a girl and meet you there. The guy always picks up the girl. I leave and come back and he'll never have to know who my date is."

Justin thought a minute. "It might work. My school's all the way across town from where you live."

"And anywhere Dad hangs out. Which is on base, and not much else."

"Okay, let's do it. I'll get the football tickets and the dance tickets on Monday and take my suit to be cleaned."

"I'll go shopping for a new jacket and pants. Where's a good place?"

"Goldstein's. If you can afford it." He leaned over and gave Clay a smacking kiss. "The more I think about it, the more I like it. It's gonna work. We should have thought of it a month ago."

"Yep. We'll make it work." Clay laughed nervously. "Dad will never know. At least, I hope not." He was quite a minute. "If you want, you could do the same thing."

"No, I couldn't. Mom volunteers at school. She'll probably be at the football game, and maybe even the dance. Besides, I don't need to." At least he hoped he didn't. Russell's comments had him wondering. But his mother would be in his corner. Still, it wouldn't hurt to give them a head's up.

He and Clay exchanged a few more fiery kisses before he headed home. The only cars in the driveway were his mom's and Russell's and he found them cleaning up the kitchen. Mindy was eating a bowl of ice cream. "You want to kill the party food?" Delores gestured to the storage cartons on the counter. "We made a meal of it tonight."

"Nah, I got tacos. How'd your meeting go?"

"Well. We got a lot nailed down," Delores said.

"Anything important?" he asked, hoping he sounded casual.

"Nothing that wasn't pretty evident to begin with," Russell said. "So, are you hanging with us for a reason or have you changed your mind about the food?"

"Kind of. I wanted to talk to you about Homecoming."

"That's coming up soon. Have you bought your tickets and ordered a corsage? Do you need some money?" his mother asked.

"Not exactly. It's about my date." Justin hesitated. Damn, this was harder than he thought it'd be.

"Who are you taking? A girl from school or one of the girls from the Academy?" Russell asked.

He took a deep breath. "Actually, I'd like to take Clay Bustamante."

His mother and stepfather both froze. Mindy put down her spoon and stared at him.

"Clay? Why would you want to take one of your buddies?" Delores asked. "Don't you want to take a date?"

"That's who I want to be my date. Clay. I want to go with Clay."

They stared at him a minute. "You want to take another boy to Homecoming *as your date*." Russell practically spat the words.

"You know I've been seeing a lot of him."

"But you're only friends," his mother protested.

"Come on, Mom. You know I'm like I am. You'd have to know," he said quietly.

"Suspected. But didn't know." Delores glanced across the kitchen at Russell, who shook his head. "This wouldn't be the time to go public with it."

"Why not?" Justin pressed.

"Don't be stupid," Russell snapped. "Your mother's running for public office. The last thing she needs is to have her cock-sucking kid show up at Homecoming holding the hand of another little fag."

Justin stared at Russell in shock. "Did you call me a cocksucker? A fag? What happened to all the tolerance you've preached over the years?" he squeaked. "The ideals you cherish so dearly?"

"Sometimes you have to soft-pedal certain beliefs when you enter the public arena," Delores said. "This is one of those times. If you want to go to Homecoming, ask a girl. Or go alone. Don't take the boy."

Justin looked from his mom to Russell. "So you're going to dump everything you've ever said you believed, and I'm supposed to stay in the closet so you can win an election." He looked at them both in horror. "Doesn't that violate every damn thing you've spent eighteen years trying to teach me?"

"You got it, kid. You're not destroying your mother's lifelong dream of holding public office. Keep your mouth shut about the gay crap and we'll be fine." Russell stared at him implacably.

"And if I don't?"

Russell's fist came out of nowhere. Justin's eye exploded in pain and he fell back on the kitchen table, knocking Mindy's ice cream to the floor. "That's what." Russell glared down at him. "You can either knuckle under or get the hell out of this house."

Justin shook the spots out from in front of his eyes. He pushed himself up from the table and looked over at his mother, who looked back at him silently. For the first time in his life, his mother betrayed him. That, more than anything, shook him to his core.

Mindy put her hands on his shoulders. "You gonna be all right?" she asked as she glared at Russell.

"Good to know where your loyalties are, mom," he muttered. His head still spinning, he went up to his room, trying to wrap his head around what'd happened.

He put a cold, wet washcloth over his throbbing eye and laid down on his bed. He'd been stupid in the extreme. He'd been so determined to get Clay to deal with his father, he hadn't thought his mother would put her political aspirations over her son. He should've known. He'd overheard enough.

They'd gone crazy. They would've had to for Russell to hit him and Mom to let him get away with it. Russell had never raised his hand to either of his stepchildren, but he sure as hell had tonight. And he'd issued Justin an ultimatum. *Knuckle under or get the hell out.*

Fuck.

Justin rewet the washcloth and considered his options. It would be the easiest thing in the world to knuckle under. Do what Russell said. Tell Clay their date was off. Keep their relationship under wraps. Clay would totally understand. Justin was tempted. But he wanted to take Clay to Homecoming. He wanted the world, or at least his friends at school, to know about his boyfriend. It meant that much to him.

Clay meant that much to him.

But it was more than Clay. He was tired of living a lie. He was tired of sneaking around. He was tired of having to think before he opened his mouth. He was tired of pretending to ogle girls when it was the guys he was interested in.

He wanted the freedom to be who he was.

If he stayed in this house, he could never do it. He'd have to remain in the closet for the sake of his mother's candidacy. He'd have to keep on living a lie. Staying here was out. It was too high a price to pay.

He'd take Clay to Homecoming even if he had to live in a cardboard box under a freeway bridge.

He packed a few things in his duffel, and when picked up his car keys, he examined them, then tossed them on the bed. The car was his mother's, and he had no right to take it. He paid for the phone himself, so he put it in his pocket. He pulled on a windbreaker and slipped out of the house, his duffel over his shoulder.

Cool wind blew in his face and lifted the hair from his forehead. He walked to the end of the block and to the entrance to the subdivision. He left the neighborhood and walked for hours, his eye throbbing and his head pounding, thinking about where to go from here.

He was kind of up shit's creek. He supposed he could contact his father, but the last he'd heard the man had remarried and was raising a second family. Not likely he'd welcome him with open arms. His grandmother was dealing with dementia and didn't need him under her feet. He could talk to the guidance counselor at school on Monday, but she'd probably tell him to make nice with his mom and stepfather and go back to the house, which was no longer home.

He'd probably end up homeless.

He wondered what spin Diego and the precinct biggies would put on that.

He sat on a curb in front of a winking bank sign, wincing when it flashed 12:43. He looked around. He didn't recognize a single building or business. Shit, he'd walked miles and was in an iffy neighborhood, far from anywhere he knew. He needed to get off the street. There was a fleabag motel down the block, but the last time he looked, he has less than twenty dollars in his wallet, and that was before he bought tacos.

He put his head in his hands. He could sleep behind the dumpster and hope nobody rolled him. Or he could use common sense and get help. But from who? There weren't too many people he could call, but the name that came to him was the same one he'd been thinking about all evening.

He'd call Clay.

Clay would help him.

He got out his phone and scrolled down to Clay's number. The phone rang three times and Justin was about to give up when a sleepy sounding Clay answered. "You okay? It's nearly one."

"No, I'm not okay." Tears welled in Justin's eyes. "Far from it. Can you come get me? Please?"

Chapter Five

Clay pulled up to the stop sign and peered down at his phone. Another two blocks. He looked both ways and went on down the deserted street, shaking his head as he passed boarded up strip centers covered with graffiti. He wondered for the hundredth time what the hell Justin was doing here, miles from home. Justin hadn't said much other than that he'd walked halfway across town and didn't have the money for a motel. He'd asked Clay for a loan so he could get a room, but no way was Clay letting him stay in the dump down the block. He'd raided his stash and brought enough money to put Justin up in a decent hotel. From what Justin said, going home wasn't an option.

Or Clay could take him to Bear's house.

He drove slowly down another block and spotted Justin sitting on a curb. He pulled over as his boyfriend stood and ran to the truck. The overhead light went on and Clay gasped at the shiner swelling Justin's eye nearly shut. "What the hell happened?"

Justin winced. "Difference of opinion with Russell."

"Russell? What the fuck?"

Justin snapped on his seat belt. "It was about you."

"Me?" Clay set his GPS for home and started down the street.

"I made the mistake of thinking they'd be okay with me taking you to Homecoming. Tolerant and broad-minded, you know. Apparently winning an election takes precedence. I was told to either shut up and knuckle under or get out of the house."

"And got cold-cocked in the process."

"Yep." Justin muttered. "I didn't even say no. All I did was ask *what if I didn't.*"

"Shit. Sounds like they mean it."

"They do."

"Why are they so vehement about you coming out? I thought you said they were tolerant."

"Russell and the precinct chairman think being sympathetic to gay causes will hurt her with the military and retired military in our district."

"So you're a gay cause now?"

"Guess so."

Clay turned the corner and pulled onto the expressway. "You could've gone along with them. I would've understood."

"I know, but I couldn't. I want to take you to Homecoming. I want the world to know you're my boyfriend."

"It's more than me and Homecoming, isn't it?"

"Yeah, it is. I'm tired of living a lie. I want to be who I am, and I want to start as I mean to go, which means taking you to Homecoming. If I get kicked out, so be it. You're worth it."

"I see."

"Did you bring some money for a hotel room?"

"Yeah, there's a bunch of nice places a couple of blocks from the house."

They fell silent. Clay glanced across the seat at Justin's shiner. It took real courage for Justin to walk out of his home. He could've taken the easy route, but he hadn't because he thought Clay was "worth it."

If Justin thought Clay was worth it, maybe he needed to start *being* worth it.

Clay glanced down at the GPS and took the Austin Highway exit. Justin looked around. "I know the area. There's a bunch of motels along here. Find one with a vacancy sign and drop me there."

Clay ignored Justin. He drove into his subdivision and pulled into the driveway of the home Bear bought for its proximity to Fort Sam. Justin looked up at the house. "I thought you had the money for a hotel room."

"I do, and we both may be in it by the end of the night."

"Huh?"

"I can't let you do this alone. If you're willing to get hit in the face for me, the least I can do is be honest about you."

"Oh, hell, no," Justin said. "If I got hit in the face, no telling what your dad will do to you."

"I guess I'm about to find out." Clay hated the quiver in his voice.

They walked up the sidewalk together. The front porch light was on and his father's imposing figure stood in the door. "Did you get your friend home?" Bear asked.

"Not exactly. I brought him home with me. Dad, this is Justin."

Bear moved aside to let the boys in. "Jesus Christ, what happened to your face?" Bear asked as Justin stepped into the foyer.

"My stepfather hit me."

"I see." Bear motioned to the family room and followed them in. Clay pulled Justin down onto the sofa and sat beside him. Bear sat in his recliner, wide awake. He looked from Justin to Clay and back to Justin, and his eyes narrowed.

He knows.

His father had taken one look at the two of them together and figured it out.

Fear squeezed Clay's heart and he wondered how long it would be before he had a one-way ticket to Singapore.

Bear steepled his hands in front of him. "So what happened? Does your stepfather abuse you regularly?"

Justin looked over at Clay. Clay nodded and squeezed his hand. "No, Colonel Bustamante, he doesn't. Never before. I made him mad tonight."

Bear waited as silence gripped the room. "Dad," Clay choked out. "It was over me. Justin told them he wants to take me to Homecoming as his date." He felt his face flush.

Bear turned to Clay. "You want to go?"

Clay swallowed. "Yes sir, I do." *If he was going to get his ass kicked out, it would be about now.*

"Hmm." Bear turned back to Justin. "Any particular reason he reacted so negatively?"

"Yes, sir. Mom's making a run for City Council and Russell thinks it will hurt her in the election if I come out."

"Who's your mother?"

"Delores Aldrich."

Bear nodded. "Not sure I get it. She and your stepfather are known liberals."

"Well, it's uh—" Justin turned a fiery shade of red.

"Mr. and Mrs. Aldrich think having a gay son will cost her with the military voters. They live close to Lackland and have a lot of military folks in her district."

"Gotcha." Bear made a production of looking at his watch. "Gentlemen, it's nearly two in the morning and we're not going to solve any of this tonight. Clay, you go on to bed. I want to talk to Justin for a few minutes, and then I'll put him up in the guest room. We'll get this sorted in the morning."

The boys nodded and Clay headed to his bedroom. He wasn't sure what to make of Bear's reaction. His father hadn't seemed to care about learning his son was gay. But then, it might've been a courtesy in front of Justin. It might be a whole 'nother story tomorrow when Justin left. Or his father might not care.

Clay didn't know Bear well enough to know.

He'd find out tomorrow.

He stripped down to his underwear and lay down. He could hear the murmur of voices coming from down the hall and wondered what Justin and his father were talking about. A few minutes later he heard his father show Justin to the spare room, and then heard the footsteps as Bear made his way to his bedroom.

Clay wondered if Justin would seek him out, but when Justin shut the door to the spare bedroom, Clay turned over and closed his eyes.

The smell of coffee woke him a few hours later. The sun was shining bright, and he could hear his dad's favorite country station playing in the background. He wandered to the kitchen where he found Bear making bacon and eggs. "Is Justin up yet?" his dad asked.

"Door's still shut, so I guess not." He made a cup of coffee and started setting places at the breakfast bar. "I'm sorry we kept you up last night," he offered tentatively. He didn't know what else to say, whether he should mention the rhinoceros on the end stool or wait until Justin was gone. Cowardice won and he sipped his coffee quietly while he worked.

Bear was dishing up the eggs when Justin appeared. His shiner looked even worse this morning and Clay stifled a wince. Justin's eyes were shadowed and he looked way older and wearier than any eighteen-year-old should. "You want coffee?" Clay asked.

Justin nodded and Clay pointed to the coffee maker on the counter. "Thanks." Bear gestured to a stool and dished up a plate of food for Justin and another for Clay before sitting down with his own. They ate in silence. Clay didn't know what to say and it was probably the same with the other two.

Finally Bear pushed his plate away and looked at Justin. "You think any more about what we talked about last night?" Justin nodded. "Okay. Guess it's time to call your mother. Go get a shower in case you have to go downtown."

Downtown? What *had* they talked about last night?

Clay had showered and shaved by the time the doorbell rang. He went to answer the door, but Bear beat him to it and introduced himself to the Aldriches, careful to include his rank. Clay's lips twitched. His dad was intimidating enough in pajama pants and a t-shirt, but this morning he was dressed for work in his DCU's and combat boots and wore what Clay thought of as his Army expression. Either he was working today, or he was forestalling any further punches.

Maybe both.

The Aldriches came in. Justin's mother, a thin woman with long hair and thick glasses, looked uncertainly from Justin to Clay. Russell looked at Clay with disdain before lasering in on Justin. If the nerdy-looking ass had any remorse for giving Justin a shiner, it didn't show.

Bear shut the front door and motioned them into the family room. "Have a seat," he said to the Aldriches. He looked at them expressionlessly, and they knew it wasn't a request.

The Aldriches sat.

Bear went to his chair and motioned for Justin and Clay to take the bean bag chairs. They sat for a moment before Russell turned to Justin. "Are you ready to stop this gay shit and see reason?" he asked.

Justin looked to Bear who nodded almost imperceptibly, then looked back at Russell. "No, sir. I'm ready to go downtown to SAPD and press charges for violating Texas Penal Code section twenty-two o-one, or as most folks say, assault and battery."

So that's what Justin and Bear had been talking about last night.

"You're *what?*" Russell demanded. He jumped up and leaned over the coffee table.

"You can't do that," his mother screeched. "You *can't*. You don't know what something like that would do to my candidacy."

"Sit down, Mr. Aldrich," Bear said firmly.

Russell took one look at Bear and sat back down.

"Actually, I can and will." Justin stared at them. "Russell hit me in the face, and knocked me across the table. He left a big purple souvenir of his temper-tantrum. You stood there and watched him do it, didn't try to stop him, and didn't say a thing afterwards. So yeah, I can and I will press charges. I was injured intentionally."

"Only after you insisted on taking your boyfriend to Homecoming," Russell said. "Look, if you want me to say I'm sorry, all right. Fine. I apologize. But if you come out, if you take him to Homecoming, it will derail your mom's chance of ever holding office. No way are the military people in our district going to vote for her if they think she's into gays." He turned to Bear. "Tell him, Mr.-uh-Colonel Bustamante. Tell him what would happen. Tell him how the men of the military feel about gays."

Bear shrugged. "We like 'em fine."

Delores looked at him disbelievingly. "Colonel, with all due respect, do you honestly expect us to believe that? Please have the decency to be honest."

"I am being honest." Bear's tone was calm and even. "We could care less. If I'm about to rout a nest of insurgents out of a safe house in some Afghan hellhole, I don't give a shit who the soldier next to me sleeps with. All I care about is if he has my six. Every soldier, marine, or SEAL who's ever gone into battle feels the same damned way. I promise you. *We don't care* who's sleeping with who."

"If you say so," she said doubtfully.

"Mr. Aldrich?" Bear asked. "Make sense to you?"

"In battle, sure. How about once they're off the battlefield?" Russell scoffed. "How did you feel when they could marry?"

"I congratulated my master sergeant on his engagement to his longtime boyfriend. Look, I don't know what kind of Neanderthals you think we are, but you're both full of crap." He glanced over at Justin. "If homophobia's rearing its ugly head, at least be honest about it. Don't blame it on your military constituents, who, by the way, *don't* like people who hit their kids. Sure would be a shame if Justin pressed charges and that little tidbit got out."

Delores and Russell sat silently until she turned to Justin. "I believe you've made your point," she said tightly. "As has the colonel. You want to take the young man to Homecoming, take him. I'm not stopping you."

Russell looked at the floor. "It's not homophobia, Colonel. It's...never mind." He got up and slammed out of the house.

Bear looked at Justin's mother. "You and your husband need to think about things," he told her. "As does Justin. He's welcome to stay with Clay and me for a few days. I'm sure Clay would love to have him."

Delores nodded. "Thank you." She turned to Justin. "I'll be in touch."

She followed her husband out the door. Justin turned to Bear. "Thank you, sir. I appreciate the support."

Bear nodded solemnly. "It was the least I could do."

"I'm not sure anything was settled, though," Clay said.

"I wouldn't worry about it," Bear said. "Justin's mother will come around. She's a little blinded by election fever, but she loves her boy, and eventually she'll decide her principles matter. Now, the stepdad? Once an asshole, always an asshole, I'm afraid."

Justin took one look at Bear's dancing eyes and burst out laughing. "You nailed it, sir."

"I'm glad that's out of the way." Clay looked at Bear sadly. "I'm sorry I disappointed you." His father's face sobered. "Really sorry. I didn't want you to know. I wasn't gonna let on. I was gonna pretend I was going to Homecoming with a girl. But when he got hit because he wanted to take me, I couldn't let him go it alone. I had to stand beside him."

Justin looked from Clay to Bear. "I'll be in the other room." He started to rise.

"No, don't run off. I have a few things to say to Clay, and it wouldn't hurt you to hear them." Justin sat down and looked at Clay apprehensively. Bear leaned forward. "Clay, we need to get a few things clear. I'm not disappointed in you. Not one damned bit. About anything."

"But I'm gay," Clay choked. "Your only son's gay."

"Yeah, you're gay. I've known for a while. Your mom mentioned it when she called me and asked if you could come here, not that either of us gives a damn. I was beginning to wonder if you were ever going to say anything about it."

"Oh." Well shit. All those times his father sat in front of the TV calling bullshit was because he thought all the politicians were talking out their ass. Clay hadn't known his old man at all.

"Far from being disappointed or hurt, I'm proud of you. Proud of both of you. You, Justin, for having the courage to stand up for yourself. Clay, you had the balls to stick by him even though you thought you were going to disappoint me. You both showed real bravery. More than it took me to go into battle."

"Oh, no, sir," Justin murmured.

Clay felt himself flush. "Not really, Dad."

"Yes, really." He smiled at them. "You're braver than you realize." His smile faded. "But as proud as I am, at the same time I'm worried. By living your lives openly, you have to know, this is only the first of many battles you'll have to fight for the right to be who you are. You won't get hit in the face every day, but it will be an uphill battle." He looked from Clay to Justin. "You need to understand that. You need to ask yourselves if you're ready."

The guys looked at one another. "If Clay has my six, I am," Justin said softly.

"And if Justin has mine, I am. You, too, Dad. I'll need you there too."

"I have your six, and I always will. Don't forget it. And on that note, duty calls." He heaved himself up. "I probably can get off early enough to take y'all to the new all-you-can-eat down the way. See you later." He disappeared out the front door.

Justin huffed, "Well damn. I wish I had a father like him."

Clay put his arm around Justin. "I knew my dad was awesome, but I didn't know until today how awesome he really is."

"You're lucky." Justin smiled crookedly.

"I am. I have an awesome dad, I have an amazing boyfriend, and I'm going to Homecoming with him." He pulled Justin close and gave him a hard, swift kiss. "What more could a guy want?"

HOLD THE LINE

Kitty Bardot

When people think of football, they think of crisp autumn nights, bonfires, hot cocoa, and warm hoodies. No one thinks of summer training camp. Of running until you fall, sweating until you puke, and slamming your body into another person repeatedly until you're both bruised and broken. That's where I am now. Lying in the grass of the practice field, sweat soaking my t-shirt. Broken. Coach is stalking this way. I can see his shadow approaching. Hear his exasperated breath, his whistle. "Get up Terry. What was that?" He's shouting again. "Get your tubby ass off the ground. Get back up and get to running."

I can't. My head feels swollen, my face hot. I can smell my acrid bile cooking in the late morning sun. His ugly face hovers above me, spittle landing on my cheeks. "Get up and catch up tubby. You're lucky you're big, cause you're the damn slowest thing I've ever seen."

"I'm sorry coach," I force out the words, every one a pulsing pain in my forehead. The tears hover behind my eyelids. *There's no crying in football. Get your ass up.*

I roll to my stomach and force myself onto my knees. I can see the rest of my team running in the distance. A couple of the slower guys glancing my way, thankful they aren't me. Chris is several paces ahead of them all, running like it's a dance. He's bare-chested with the rest of the skilled guys. They're built for running, for throwing, for catching, and for being shirtless. Not me. I'm a wall. Built to stop and keep safe. Built to stand strong and hold the line while Chris and the others maneuver and score.

As I get up off the ground, the August heat shimmers around me. Coach, looking up from a good six inches beneath me sneers. "Does your dad know you can't run a single lap without puking and crying?"

"It's so hot," I choke out in response as the spiraling ache swirls in my gut again. We've been at it since eight in the morning and it was already hot then. As I try to focus on his face, growing redder by the moment, I feel that same lurch again. What little bile I have left lands on coach's polo and spatters his cheek. His eyes bulge, the vein in his forehead pulses.

"Get the hell off of my field," he growls through clenched teeth. "I want you here at six tomorrow morning. If you're too much of a princess to run in the heat, you're going to run twice as much."

"Yes coach." I nod horrified I vomited on our coach in front of the whole team. *I'll never hear the end of it.*

The cold air in the locker room hits my sweat-soaked clothes. The relief is brief. My face still burns, my body aches. It's too cold. I start to shiver uncontrollably. Peeling the wet shirt and shorts away, I'm thankful it's only me and my reflection, and I wish what I see would disappear. I pull my beach towel from my locker. A standard size towel doesn't cover me. All I want is to be covered. I think of the guys out on the field, their slim waists and sculpted muscles. Their sun-kissed melanin richness. Even the white guys have color. Not me. My skin barely sees the sun. My muscles hide under layers of fat, layers that no matter how hard I diet, how little I eat, never budge. I'm a wall. That's my job. I'm here to stand between Chris and the other team. I'm here to stop the other guys. There's no glory in that.

Glory is what my dad had in mind when he named me Terry after the greatest quarterback of his time. I'm no quarterback. Dad accepted it when I hit six feet at thirteen. I'm not built for skill or speed. I'm built for strength. Lucky for Dad, Chris moved in next door with no dad of his own and plenty of skill. I'll never forget the day he popped his head over the fence holding the football I'd thrown haphazardly into his yard. Dad's eyes lit up as Chris chucked an effortless spiral right into his waiting hands. The glory Dad had been expecting from me was transferred to Chris with one perfectly placed pass. Chris became a permanent fixture at our house, and as much as I wanted to hate him, I couldn't. It'd been a relief to be free from my dad's ever-present training, and strict dietary guidelines. He didn't judge my second helpings or my thirds anymore. He let me sleep a little later on the weekends. And more often than not, the unrelenting passing back and forth had turned into me watching him and Chris tossing the ball from the porch while I munched on some fresh baked cookies. Mom makes the best cookies.

The thought of Mom's cookies gives my stomach another lurch. I don't need food right now. I need water, a shower, some clean clothes, and a nap. I hurry to the showers, eager to be in and out before the rest of the guys get here. My feet slap and stick to the cement floor. The water runs tepid from the showerhead, and runs through my hair, down over my shoulders and back. My tears flow freely. No one can see me crying in the shower. The water cools my burning face. I open my mouth and swallow about a gallon, but my head's still buzzing. Me and heat have never been friends. I hate football.

"Hey, big guy," Ben calls from the doorway. Laughter floats across the shower room. It's friendly laughter. You don't have bullies when you're the biggest.

"Fuck off," I grunt at them all. Several pairs of bare feet appear around me as the various showerheads run. The feet are attached to shapely legs, made for running. This is where it gets awkward. *Keep your eyes down.* I tell myself. *Don't look up.* I recognize their voices. I know whose smiling faces I'll see, whose rippling abs and rounded pecs. I know their cocks will be hanging slack and happy between their legs. They're none the wiser how difficult these moments are. I love to see them like this, wet and glistening, relaxed and on display. Their bodies bare, their sculpted asses. "I'm out of here." I keep my eyes averted. "Coach wants me back at six in the morning."

"You should've seen his face when you puked on him." Sam laughs from the far shower head.

"Yeah." I give an offhanded chuckle and hurry away, wrapping my towel around my waist.

***

Six in the morning on the practice field. The grass is cool and wet with dew. Coach isn't here. I didn't expect to see him. He knew I'd be here. Always the obedient one. Always on time. How often had he looked at me with disdain, saying something about how he wished the skilled guys had my dedication? How often had I overheard him and my dad discuss my drive and what a pity it was that I didn't have *it*?

Grateful for the quiet morning, for the moment without Coach or Dad watching my every move, I jog slowly around the track, the weight of each step jarring my body. The air is already warm and sticky. Sweat runs freely down my back.

"Hey, big guy," Chris calls as he jogs up beside me. My heart skips in my chest.

"Hey," I respond between labored breaths. "What are you doing here?"

"I figured you could use some company," he says.

"Thanks." I struggle to keep my voice as level as his.

"You've taken so many hits for me. It's the least I can do."

"You're the man with the ball."

"Yeah. Well, you're the one who keeps it that way." He offers a gleaming smile of perfect white teeth, displaying the irresistible dimple, which creases his cheek when he gives his most genuine grins. We run together with only the sound of our feet on the track and the birds in the trees. The sun creeps higher in the sky, threatening to have its way with me again. "We missed you at the drive-in last night. You wouldn't believe how real Godzilla looked. It's crazy what they can do with computers," he says as we round the bend.

"I wasn't feeling it." I keep my response calm though my emotions are running wild. *He missed me.*

"I believe that. I hate how hard Coach pushes you. It always seems like he singles you out."

"I know. I think he and my dad have some sick agreement to torture me. Makes me wonder what I did in a past life to deserve their punishment."

"You don't deserve any of it, man. I hate the way he's always shitting on you."

"I'm used to it." I shrug, my eyes on the track ahead of me, each lumbering footfall shaking my tired bones.

He slows down and stops jogging. I do the same. His dark eyes twinkle in the morning light. "It really wasn't the same without you last night," he says. For a brief moment I convince myself he's trying to say something more. That his missing me at the drive-in is his secret way of telling me he loves me. "Molly and Steph were there. They're so hot." He shakes his head and laughs a bit. "Wish they weren't so annoying. Steph was asking about you."

"Yeah?"

"I think she wants a piece of the Terry bear."

"Whatever." I laugh through my nose. "C'mon let's get back to it. Coach could be here any minute." I know it's not like that. I know he won't ever look at me the way he looks at Molly and Steph and all the other girls. In moments like this, however, I can convince myself I mean something to him, and I'm special in a way. If only he knew how special he was to me.

***

People make room for me in the halls. They step aside to let me pass. The girls smiling, the guys clapping my back. The underclassmen scurry out of my way. On game days I wear the number sixty-six with pride. The guys joke that my jersey had to be specially made. Yet, they're sure thankful for the size of that jersey when I'm standing between them and the rushing defense. The cheerleaders smile but they never bat their eyes the way they do at Chris and the others. I'm like a teddy bear, they say. They love my hugs. Some fellas might be upset by it. I don't mind. The girls are sweet, pretty too. If I were the slightest bit interested it might hurt to know they see me as a harmless teddy bear. It might hurt to see them fawn over the more fit and handsome guys on the team. I understand though. Those guys are beautiful. Chris in particular. It's not only his good looks and perfect build. It's his heart as well. He shines with a light from within that can't be ignored. He's a real *rescue a kitten from a burning building while helping an old lady across the street* kind of guy. He'd do it all with humble grace and hair perfectly mussed. Probably a bit of ash streaked across his cheek.

"Terry," a soft, feminine voice calls from an open doorway. I turn to see Ms. Pharris standing there with her wild hair and oversized glasses. "Do you have a minute?"

"Sure." I shrug. She steps aside to let me pass then closes the door behind her. It's weird. Her door is never closed.

"This won't take too long. I can write you a hall pass if you need one. Sit, please." She brushes past me, her long skirt fluttering as she moves. A cloud of sweet perfume follows.

"What's up?" I ask, settling onto the desktop as she pulls my notebook off of a stack on her desk.

"This," she says waving it slightly with a look of shock on her mousy face.

"I'm sorry, Ms. Pharris. I'm not a writer. I don't know what I'm doing."

"That's where you're wrong, Terry. You have an extraordinary gift. These poems have more heart and soul than any I've seen in a long time."

"Really?" My heart does a weird sort of flip. My cheeks warm. I've never been told I had any gift other than my size. It feels good until she opens the journal and leans against her desk before me. As she starts to read my heart does a nose dive right into my stomach. The embarrassment of hearing my words makes my ears burn.

"Silent... Still... Unrequited is my love. Never to dance in the halls of my heart. Never to rise as blush upon my cheek. Never to sing its name upon my soul. Never... to...be." The cadence of her voice is over the top, pretentious. She stares at me through her magnifying glass lenses, her eyes are huge, cartoonish. "This is beautiful Terry." She gives her head a subtle shake and thumbs through my journal. "Everything in here is beautiful. You have such a way with words." She looks to be ready to read another one. I stand, my face still burning. Images of Chris in my mind, running beside me on the track, catching passes in my yard, eating across from me at lunch. Every word in that book is inspired by him.

"Thanks, Ms. Pharris. I guess I do know what I'm doing then." I start to move, cutting off any more potential embarrassment. I can't possibly hear her read another one.

"No, thank you. These were a wonderful surprise." She holds my notebook to her chest.

"I'm glad you liked them." It's an awkward moment as she stares at me in silence.

"I have a request. I'd like to publish some of these in our annual literary mag. The kids in journalism put one together every year. Would you be okay with that?" My cheeks are burning again. I don't want the whole school to read my words. I don't know why I ever wrote them, and worse, why I turned them in. I'll never hear the end of it.

"I'd rather you not." My voice is smaller than I intended, it squeaks out through my throat swelling with emotion.

Ms. Pharris cocks her head and blinks. "I'm sorry. I suppose I should have considered the deep connection you have with your poetry. When you're writing with this level of passion it can be difficult to let the world see. I can assure you though, anyone who reads your words will be moved."

"My dad won't. Coach won't. My team won't." My words fall like rocks between us. "I'd rather not have it out there for everyone to see."

She takes a deep breath and pulls herself up as tall as she can, still looking up. "I hate football." The bell rings. She drops my journal unceremoniously onto her desk and walks around bending to fill out a hall pass. "If you change your mind, the deadline isn't until December. You have a real talent here. It would be a shame to squander it." She hands me the small slip of yellow paper with a tight-lipped smile. "Good luck tonight."

"Thanks." I take the slip and leave. The halls are quiet. Her words sink in. No one has ever said I had a talent for anything. If Dad could trade me for Chris, I'm sure he would in a heartbeat. I can't blame him though. I'd do the same.

Stephanie turns the corner. Her red and white cheerleading uniform is almost indecent. She smiles, brightly bouncing my way. "Hey, Terry Bear," she says as she stands on tiptoes and wraps her arms around my neck. "You have a date for Homecoming yet?"

"I wasn't planning on going." I give her a gentle squeeze in return. She smells like flowers and peaches.

"You can't miss Homecoming. It's senior year." She slips from my arms and walks beside me.

I shrug. "I'm okay with it."

"But you're on the court." She stops walking and places her hands on her hips.

"Don't remind me." I turn to face her, rolling my eyes.

"I'm glad I did. You have to be there."

"Who says?"

"I don't know." She shrugs. "Everyone."

"Are you asking me to Homecoming then?" I tease. Girls don't ask me on dates.

"Well actually, yeah."

"Really?" I laugh, surprised.

"Yes, really. We're the only ones on the court who don't have dates. I figured we might as well go together. Plus, Chris is already going with Molly. I thought it would be fun for the four of us."

I look her over. Her thick blonde hair is combed into a high, tight ponytail. Her makeup is flawless. Her uniform looks like she was poured into it in the best way possible. Most guys would fall at her feet and happily beg for a date. "How do you not have a date already?"

She looks down at her sneakers then back to me with a shrug. "Ever since I broke up with Ben, he's been threatening every guy I talk to. He can't threaten you though." She smiles and bats her eyes. "You're three times his size."

"Thanks, I think."

"Oh, come on. Just as friends? You can tell him we're friends. I have to go and I don't want to go alone. You're like my only option at this point." Her voice goes up an octave or two as she tilts her head to one side. "Ben's being such an asshole. He has a date already. I don't know why he cares if I do."

I shake my head, unable to come up with a solid reason to refuse. "Ben *is* an asshole," I offer with a smile. I've never understood why he had such a chip on his shoulder. He's a running-back who can't hold onto the ball. Nothing to be proud of there. He does look damn good in the uniform though, and that's more than I can say for myself.

"So, you'll go with me?"

I look down at her eager face. She's always been a friend, genuinely happy to greet me with open arms and a smile. "Sure. Why not?"

She brightens instantly and stretches to wrap her arms around my neck again, planting a kiss on my cheek. "Oh, thank you." She slides down my chest and gives me another squeeze before heading away. "I'm going to tell Molly. Chris is going to be so happy. It was his idea to ask you."

His idea? It's about as close to him asking me as I'll ever get. My mind wanders to a distant future when someone like me can walk the halls proudly. Not because of the jersey on my back, but for the song in my heart. Instead of running until I puke and beating up myself and others up on the field, I could write and daydream, and walk with the girls with their soft laughter and sweet scents. We could giggle and tell secrets about the boys we like. Stephanie would never ask me to double date with Chris because she'd know what he meant to me. Even though he didn't. It's an imaginary future though. In the meantime, I settle for the crumbs of what might be.

They must know on some innate level I'm different. There is nothing to fear from my six foot four, three-hundred-pound frame. They know I'm soft. They know I'm gentle. They come to me with teary eyes and broken hearts asking for advice.

There is no one for me though.

No one I can tell my deepest secrets to.

***

Friday morning, we gather in our second-best clothes outside the auditorium. The homecoming court ready to parade through the crowd and be applauded. For what, I don't know. Stephanie is on my arm, looking radiant. Chris and Molly are behind us. Everyone knows they'll be crowned king and queen.

"You clean up nice, big guy," Chris calls from behind. I turn to see him. I look like a used-car-salesmen in my black shirt and red tie. He looks immaculate in his black shirt and thin white tie.

"Yeah. You too." I laugh and do my best not to let my gaze linger on his slim waist and flat stomach. "You look great, Molly," I offer looking over her tight-fitting black dress.

"Wait 'til you see us tomorrow," she says with a proud grin, pulling Chris closer possessively. He makes a face for me she can't see. One that says *help*. I snort in response. "What?" she asks angrily.

"Nothing." I shake my head and turn back toward the door. We're about to begin the foolish parade.

"What's he laughing at?" I hear her ask Chris as we begin the procession.

"You two." Stephanie, having watched the exchange shakes her head. "Thanks for doing this," she says softly squeezing my arm.

"No problem."

Applause fills the room as each couple is announced. Everyone receiving their recognition for winning the high school popularity game. "Terry Moore and Stephanie Little," Principal Smith says in his monotone voice. The crowd cheers wildly as we walk by, giving us more love than the couples before us.

It feels good to be seen and celebrated. I can't help but wonder if they would cheer so loudly if they knew who I *really* am. If they knew I dreamed about Chris every night and longed for a world where it was okay to love him, a world where he loved me back.

"Chris Perez and Molly Sims," the applause becomes a roar. In this world everyone loves him. I watch as they walk up the aisle. Molly beams. I wonder if she knows the applause is all for him, and how little it matters who's on his arm? Would they cheer so loudly if it were me? Possibly more, but only because it would be a joke. They'd love it as long as it wasn't real.

***

We win the homecoming game. Of course, we win. Chris is the star. I hold the line. He runs and scores. I hold the line. He passes and scores. I hold the line. He runs again. I hold the line. Each quarter of the game flies by. The lights, the grass, the bodies crushing together time and again are on repeat as we pummel the other team. There's nothing quite like the sound of two bodies running into each other at full speed. The pads and helmets smacking and crashing. Not a single body hits Chris.

Because of me.

I hold the line.

We win.

***

Dad's proud at Saturday morning at breakfast. He smiles across the table and nods as Mom places a mountain of pancakes and bacon in front of me.

"I think it's terrible," she says shaking her head picking up the conversation they'd been having before I entered the room.

"I say he had it coming." Dad huffs laying the newspaper on the table beside him. "Little queer like that should have known better." Shock runs through me, harder than two helmets smacking together. *Little queer?*

"What are you talking about?" I ask, sipping my orange juice.

"Oh, it's terrible," Mom laments, "This boy in Wyoming. He was…" she lowers her voice, "he was gay, and these men beat him and left him to die. It's been all over the news. It's the most terrible thing I've ever heard." She shakes her head and dabs at the corners of her eyes.

"Stop going on about it. One less queer for us to worry about. He probably has AIDS anyway."

Suddenly the delicious meal I was excited to eat looks like a flavorless pile.

"How can you say that?" she asks, her hand on her heart. "He was a boy. Not much older than Terry. To think what his parents must be feeling."

"Should have raised him better," Dad says. "You won't see Terry getting into that kind of trouble. Have you seen his homecoming date?" He chuckles and shovels pancakes in his mouth, giving me a wink. My hunger disappears.

Mom shakes her head in disapproval. She passes the butter and syrup my way. I dress my pancakes on autopilot. My dad's words on repeat in my mind.

"I was surprised when Steph asked me." I keep my eyes on my plate while attempting conversation.

"See." Dad chimes in. "*She* asked him. That's my boy." He opens the paper again his face disappears behind the headline.

Gay Man Attacked And Left For Dead

Beside it is a picture of a sweet-faced guy with a shy smile. A guy whose only crime was wanting his kind of love. My stomach flips and rolls. It feels like his black and white image is watching my every move.

"It's not like that." I clear my throat, looking to Mom. "We're going as friends. Me and Chris and Steph and Molly." I take a small bite of pancake. It tastes like soggy cardboard. "You know, I'm still pretty tired from the game last night. I think I need to go back to sleep. You mind if I heat this up later?"

"Are you feeling sick?" she asks. I can tell she's fighting the urge to place a hand on my forehead and check me for a temperature.

"Leave him be, dear," Dad's voice floats over the newspaper. "You've got to start treating him like the man he is. You saw him out there on the field last night, didn't you? A beast like that doesn't need his mother babying him."

She sighs and looks at Dad mostly obscured by the newspaper, shaking her head again. "Go on upstairs. I'll take care of it." She sips her coffee and pushes her plate away.

In the dark of my room, I cry quiet tears. My chest heaving as I sob. The joy of our homecoming victory short-lived. Even my dad's words of approval were tainted by the terrible things he said about the man in the headlines. The ache in my chest is unbearable. How can he have so much hate for someone he's never met? How could he say such cruel things in light of another's tragedy? Would it make a difference if he knew who I really am? What I really am?

Just another queer.

My tears eventually dry and I lie motionless, suspended in the pain that is my life.

***

"Morning sunshine." Chris stands above me, his smile gleaming. For a moment I forget the pain from breakfast. I blink the sleep away and sit up.

He sits in my desk chair in gym shorts and a ribbed tank. His bare feet look almost delicate on my plush carpet. His arm muscles move and bunch as he reaches for the football on my desk. He holds it as he speaks, tossing it from one hand to the other.

"What's up?"

"Nothing, I had to get away from my house. I swear Molly's called me at least a hundred times today." He grins and spins in the chair. His eyes sparkle with a playful glint. "I don't think I'll ever understand girls."

"Me either," I grunt, sitting up quickly to hide my second morning wood of the day, made unbearable by his presence.

"You know we should've just gone together." He chuckles innocently and my heart soars at the thought. "Would've been so much easier." The football spirals toward the ceiling then falls perfectly in his open hands. He flashes me another dimpled grin and tilts the chair back against my desk.

"Yeah, we could've stayed home."

His laughter fills the room. "For real." He stares at the ceiling. I stare at him. "You ever wonder what the point is of all this?"

"Of what?"

"High school, homecoming, fucking football." He shakes his head and drops the chair back to the ground tossing the football to the floor. "We push so hard. We try so hard. For what? To do the same thing in college for another four years until we graduate and get some shitty jobs, get married, have kids. All so they can do the same shit we're doing and wonder why they're doing it?" He shakes his head with a sneer. "I don't want to go tonight."

"Me either."

"You know, when I told Molly I would go if you would, I thought you'd say no." He snorts and picks the ball up again. "I should've said no myself. Saved us both the trouble."

"How can they have a homecoming dance without their homecoming king?" I tease.

"I don't want to be homecoming king." The phone rings.

"Terry, honey," Mom calls, "There's a Molly on the phone, she's looking for Chris."

"Looks like you don't have a choice." I laugh.

He rolls his eyes. "Guess not." He crosses the room and picks up the receiver with an exaggerated grimace.

***

We take so many pictures. First at Molly's house, Steph's parents are there. Then back to my house. Chris' mom is there too. It's Me and Steph, then Chris and Molly, then all four of us, then Molly and Steph, then, Chris and then me. We strike masculine poses, never touching. Dad throws a football into the mix. We pantomime some plays in our shirts and suspenders. Molly looks distressed we might get dirty or wrinkled. We head out in my dad's car. He slips me some cash and squeezes my shoulder.

At school there're more pictures. I'm a prop. Eight girls position themselves around me. The guys do the same. I end up cradling Chris in my arms like a princess. He drapes an arm over my shoulder. Laughter and smiles fill the room. No one knows how hard it is for me not to crush him to my chest. The intimacy of holding him in my arms breaks me apart inside.

It's all a joke though. We'll have these pictures for years to come. This one might make it in the yearbook even. Everyone will remember it well. Except, I'll see the heartbreak behind my glasses as I hold the love of my life as closely as I ever will. All for a laugh. I'll never forget the warm smell of his body as he lifts his arm over my head and hops out of my arms.

No one dances at homecoming. Not like in the movies. All the girls shake their asses in a circle under strands of twinkling Christmas lights while the guys watch from a distance. The music is so loud you have to shout to speak. Spice Girls, Sir Mix-a-Lot, and Rednex has the girls squealing. More than once, I catch an eye roll from Chris. I stand obedient, as always, waiting for the night to end. It's a hell of a lot better than football practice.

The time comes for the king and queen to be announced. No one is surprised. Chris and Molly have their dance under the disco ball. Molly's expression is the picture of adoration. She bats her eyes and bites her lower lip. She speaks softly, looking up at Chris. Chris moves through the motions, clearly bored by it all. Steph holds onto my arm pressing her body against me.

"Are we going to the after party at Sam's? I hear his parents left for the night," she says as she watches Chris and Molly.

"I suppose you want to," I respond.

"I do. It is our last homecoming after all."

"It is that."

"Let's go for a bit. If it's lame, we can leave."

"All right," I answer, knowing it's going to be lame and knowing she won't want to leave.

***

I'm sitting in a chair in Sam's basement. Several of my classmates stand in front of me around a pool table, their dress clothes rumpled, some stained. All the girls are barefoot. The music is loud. The conversations louder. I had one beer an hour ago, and haven't seen Chris for a while. Haven't seen Molly either. Chances are they're alone in a room somewhere, breaking my heart.

Steph approaches looking like she's found the bottom of the keg. "Hey, Terry Bear." She giggles and drops onto my lap. Her updo has fallen down. Her make-up faded. The strap of her red dress slips off of her shoulder. She puts it in place. It falls again. "Ben is here," she slurs. "He's here with is stupid girlfriend, and they're in Sam's parents' room right now." She takes a drink from her plastic cup.

"I'm sorry, Steph." I take the cup from her hand. "Here, let me have that." She pouts slightly, but gives it up without a fight.

"You wanna kiss me?" she asks, raising herself up to straddle my lap. Anxiety grips me as she takes my hand and places it on her cheek. She bats her lashes and pouts her lip.

"Who wouldn't?" I answer, not sure how to get out of the situation. Before I know it, her lips are on mine, sloppy and wet. She moves and wiggles against me and coos in my ear. I place my hands on her shoulders and push her away, gently. "Steph, stop." I speak as soft as I can, not wanting to draw attention to us. Unfortunately, it's too late.

"Come on, Terry Bear," she pleads, unaware of our audience. She bounces on my lap. If I were the man my dad thought I was, I'd be loving every minute of her body on mine. I'm not that man.

"People are watching," I say quietly, holding her hands in mine, trying to keep them from moving over my body.

"Let them watch." She leans in to kiss me again. "I want them to see. I want Ben to see." She plants another sloppy kiss on my lips and works her hands free from my grip sneaking one between my legs. I jump and push her away with more force than I intend. She lands like a rag doll on the floor and looks up with drunken spite. The room goes silent. A dozen faces watch with shock and awe. "You really are a faggot aren't you?" she spits her words.

I sit frozen in my seat, feeling the color drain from my face. "What?" I stammer, shaking my head looking from one face to the next.

"Everyone said you were, but I didn't believe them. Even Ben said you were. When I told him I was going to the dance with you, he said he didn't care at all because you were a fucking queer. He was right. Wasn't he?" She sneers and pulls herself up against the pool table, looking down at me. "You don't have to answer. Your little soft dick did that for you."

My heart shatters. Stephanie, who I thought was my friend, stares at me with the same disdain I saw in my dad's face at breakfast. I open my mouth to speak but nothing comes out. My throat closes on words I can't find. Tears wet the corners of my eyes.

I do my best to blink them away, but they flow freely. The room is silent. My classmates, my friends, my teammates all stare at me. Some with blank faces others with the same look of disgust. I hear Chris from behind me. His voice, normally full of good humor and charm has a cold edge.

"What the fuck, Stephanie?" He steps between her and me, blocking me from her angry glare. "Will someone take her home? She's wasted," he says to the room. Molly steps up beside her, shooting a quick look my way. The crowd begins to talk again. Someone volunteers to give her a ride. My mouth is dry. My body feels glued to the seat. Chris turns around and looks down at me. "You all right?"

"Yeah." My voice is barely a squeak. I wipe at my wet cheeks with the back of my hand.

"Let's get out of here. I'm over this." He tips his head back toward the door. His tie hangs open at his neck. He's undone his first three buttons of his shirt and rolled his sleeves to his elbows. He's picture perfect.

I can't speak so I nod and stand as quickly as I can. I can feel everyone's stares on my back as I walk away with Chris following close behind. A murmur follows as gossip spreads one whisper at a time.

Outside is quiet and peaceful. A cold wind stings my damp face. Chris speaks first as we walk along the sidewalk towards my dad's car. "That was bullshit."

I shrug and swallow over the lump in my throat. "She's drunk."

"So what? That was awful. She had no right to talk to you like that." His voice is laced with anger.

"You didn't have to leave you know."

"Man, fuck that place. Fuck that party and those people. This whole town is nothing but hicks."

We walk on the sidewalk of Sam's neighborhood. Houses loom in large yards far from us, their windows dark. Our classmates' cars line the street. I'm embarrassed, afraid of what will happen on Monday. I couldn't have handled the situation any worse than I did. If I would've stood up and called Stephanie a dumb slut, I would have been safe. Nothing she said after that would have mattered. They would have laughed at her sprawled on the floor. Instead, I choked, and I cried. Until Chris came along and saved the day. I was a cat in a burning building. He carried me away from the fire.

"Thanks man." The only words I can muster.

"For what?" he asks.

"For getting me out of there."

"No problem," he responds. It's quiet. A single cricket sings in the chilly air calling for a mate who will never answer. "You've always been there for me."

"But that stuff she said..."

"It doesn't matter."

"You know what they're going to say."

"I don't care what they're going to say. Or what they think." He stops walking and faces me. "You're my best friend. You've been there for me since the day we met. You stand between me and every meathead motherfucker who wants to crush me. You do it all and ask for nothing. You're literally the only person in my world who doesn't expect something from me. So, what if you're gay?"

My tongue lies thick and heavy in my mouth. He can't possibly know what his words mean to me. "But—"

"Stop, dude." He shakes his head. "It doesn't change a thing. Neither one of us wants to be in this town any longer than we have to be. Neither one of us should care about what any one of them thinks. We're bigger than this. We're bigger than them."

I want to hug him. I want to squeeze him to my chest and kiss his face and tell him he's my world and I'll do anything for him. "We've got less than a year before we get out of here for good. Then, we never have to look back. I hear college is where people go to be gay." He laughs. "You'll be so busy fighting off guys, you'll forget all about me. I'll be a third string quarterback daydreaming about the good old days and you'll be living your best life." He starts walking again, smiling over his shoulder.

"That's not possible," I say as we come up to the car.

"I don't know. They scout out the best, and we'll be freshmen."

"I could never forget about you." I watch for his response. He offers a humble half smile and huffs.

"We'll see about that. Want me to drive?" he asks.

"No, I'm good." As we move to open the doors, I see several of our teammates on Sam's lawn. They're making a wild amount of noise as they run toward us. I hurry around the car to Chris' side, my heart racing with fear. The headline from the newspaper running through my mind. *Could they turn on me that quickly? On Chris?*

"Fuuuuuck," Ben shouts to the sky as they approach. "Shit got so lame in there. Stephanie lost her damn mind. Where are you guys going?"

"Home," Chris answers, as he steps in front of me.

"You can't leave," Sam says from behind the others. "I know Stephanie killed the party, but we were thinking of playing some seven on seven."

"Really?" I'm shaken to my core. They are all standing there as if nothing happened. As if my deepest darkest secret hadn't been laid bare for all to see.

"Yeah really. Unless you two were gonna go make out or some shit," Ben answers. "Come on." The group runs away as quickly as they came.

"What I'd tell you?" Chris asks as we follow the rowdy bunch. "None of it matters."

"Damn Sam. You've got a huge backyard," someone calls from behind his house.

"Is your backyard big enough for Terry?" another shout, followed by rolling laughter. Chris is right. None of it matters.

"Don't worry Sam, Terry's gonna make room in your backyard."

"He'll be gentle though."

"You better hope he's gentle."

The shouts are met with cackles and jeers. I'm in awe of the moment. My teammates, my friends, they don't care. Chris and I take our time catching up with the others.

"Thanks again," I say.

"For what?"

"There was a moment there when I thought I might have to fight my way out. Then you were there, and you held the line. You said it yourself. This town is full of hicks. Hicks are great at becoming an angry mob. I'm not sure what would've happened tonight without you."

"I'd face all of the angry mobs for you man."

"Really?"

"Fuck yeah, really. You're my best friend, I love you, and I'm not afraid to say it," he assures me as we approach the gate.

"I love you too." I'm fighting tears again. New, beautiful tears, full of gratitude and joy.

"Hey Terry, you wanna be center?" Ben calls from the group gathered on the lawn.

"That's it." I shout as I charge into them. They scatter, unscathed. Our laughter rising to the stars. My heart feels light as the future I've dreamed of materializes before my eyes. I'm accepted and loved for exactly who I am. I always have been.

***

It's August and I'm lounging on a blanket in the shade. My professor sits on a lawn chair discussing Ginsburg and his views on materialism and sexual repression. My mind wanders to the fear and guilt that'd plagued me for so many years and how Chris with his kindness and courage set me on a path to leave it all behind.

Dad was pissed when I told him I was done playing football. He barely spoke to me for weeks, and still has little to say. Ms. Pharris was an amazing help once I told her I was ready to publish my poetry. Once published, she sent copies of the mag to several colleges along with a collection she helped me choose from my years of filling journals with my heart. Though the scholarships don't come rolling in for poetry like they do for football, Dad couldn't deny the value of the full rides I received from several small liberal arts schools. Mom loved my new passion, and supported it with zeal, leaving him to pout in silence more than once.

Chis went with a state school, division one. He says he's not as good of a quarterback without my help. He's lying. He might go pro. I remember the things he said that night about me forgetting him and how wrong he was. I could never forget my best friend, my first love, the guy who held the line for me when I thought everyone would turn their backs. How could I forget him?

As I look around at my new classmates, each one different from the other. I'm in a place where individual expression is celebrated. Where guys like me are free to show their true selves. A handsome dark-haired boy with sparkling blue eyes smiles at me from across the group. I don't know his name yet, but I've caught him watching me more than once. He bats his lashes and looks away, sweet and bashful. I smile back and join the conversation, thrilled about this new adventure.

I realize Chris was right.

I'm here living my best life.

SHAKE ME DOWN

Elle Wright

Everett

Everett walked into his fourth high school in three years. Between being a military brat of two high-ranking officers, and the child of a divorce where his 'rents had agreed to bounce him between whichever one of them was stateside, his ability to form lasting relationships was sketchy.

Not that he didn't want to, or hadn't tried, but being the new kid pretty much every other year of his life had made him a permanent outsider. Silver lining? Having grown up with two hard-asses, he knew how to turn circumstances to his advantage.

Over the years, he'd become the quintessential hustler. You wanted it—he found a way to get it. At a premium price, of course. Everyone assumed his 'rents had scratch, but it'd been his cash monay that'd paid for his vintage gun metal gray 1990 soft-top ZR-1 Corvette.

"Yo, Monty." Everett's last name was Montgomery, and Monty worked so much better for a hustler than Everett. "You nail down that 'special order?'"

Everett shook his head. Phillip Legrand was a fidiot. Like who the fuck yells that shit before first period in the middle of the main hallway when half the student population can hear, not to mention the teachers. He walked up to the vanilla pale white boy, wrapped his hand around the football captain's shoulder and steered the asshole into the central courtyard.

"Listen, shithead," he squeezed the fucker's shoulder hard, "you mouth-off like that again in public, and you'll be coughing up your teeth for weeks. Feel me?" The douchebucket nodded and Everett gave his shoulder another deep squeeze before he shoved Legrand away. "I told you. I'm not getting you no roofies, man."

"But you said—"

"I *said*, I could get anything anyone wanted, as long as I wanted to get it. I *don't* want to get your limp dick roofies. You can't score with the chicks on your own, that's sad, but it ain't my problem. I'm not into drugging people to get off."

By now, white boy's face had turned a mottled pinkish red and his fisted hands banged against his outer thighs. Everett crossed his arms over his chest and leaned against the wall waiting for the predictable barrage to come spewing out of the cracker's mouth.

"You fuckin' faggot." He lunged at Everett who shook his head as he ducked. When heard Legrand's fist land on the stucco wall, he turned on the balls of his feet in his squat, and then stood to see he'd gotten his wish. Legrand had thrown the punch with his passing hand. Boo-hoo. Guess who wasn't going to be playing for the rest of the season? Whoops. There went the homecoming game.

Legrand was cradling his hand against his chest while trying not to cry. "You know," Everett said through his grin, "I love being a faggot. So much better to sucked off by a dude who knows what a man needs than by a silly little girl who can't wrap her lips around the head." He looked down at Legrand's crotch and shrugged. "Maybe in your case, that's not an issue."

Turning to walk out of the courtyard to his first class before the bell rang, he wasn't worried Legrand would come after him. Hundred to one, the hand, and maybe the wrist, were broken. That had to hurt like a sonofabitch.

***

Zachary

A quarter second before the bell rang, Everett Montgomery swaggered into class looking like a wet dream. His caramel skin, his loose black curls he wore in a big 'fro, his long thick thighs tightly encased in black jeans, and his broad muscled shoulders obvious even under his black leather jacket... Holy shit. Zach had to shift in his chair to keep from breaking his throbbing dick.

The day before his senior year of high school began, Zach had set his countdown clock to graduation day. He knew it would be an endurance test, but he'd manage. He'd been invited to apply to MIT after placing in the top fifteen at the Regeneron ISEF. While he figured it was as close to a guarantee to getting in as anyone could get, he'd applied to CalTech and Stanford as a failsafe. He preferred to stay in California, but he wouldn't pass up the opportunity to go to MIT if they accepted him.

Since he was a little kid, he'd known he was a geek, and it didn't bother him. His father

was a robotics engineer, his mother was an epidemiologist, and his older sister was in her first year at Harvard medical school. Brains ran in the family. Not looks.

Zach wasn't particularly vain, but he'd love to get laid before he headed off to college, if for no other reason, he felt like he was going to explode. He'd been working up the nerve to talk to Monty—he hated that name and preferred to call him Everett—not to ask him out. Hell no. Zach was playing left field in the peewee league while Everett was the star pitcher for the San Francisco Giants. Zach figured he'd use some of his savings to pay Everett to fix him up on a date. You know, another geek who wore glasses and was into guys. He heard Everett charged extortionate prices and hoped five hundred dollars would be enough. It was all Zach was prepared to take out his personal college fund.

Everett was stuffing his big body into the seat next to Zach's, which made all the rest of the blood in his veins that wasn't already in his dick, rush down that way. He was sure he was going to faint.

"Hey," Everett whispered as Mr. Horatio took attendance the old-fashioned way, by calling out names. Zach never could figure out why since they all signed in electronically on their iPads—one of the benefits of private school—but was happy for the redundancy today because *Everett was talking to him.* "You all right, Ellis?"

Zachary Asher Ellis. The story was his great-grandfather had a long complicated Russian last name and the immigration official at Ellis Island had said, "Fuck it. Your last name is Ellis." From time to time, Zach's grandfather had grumbled, "What kind of a Jewish name is Ellis." Then he'd threaten to change their name back, but he never did. "Yep. I'm okay." He nearly croaked that out, but managed to sound semi-normal.

"You sure, man?"

Zach nodded at the same time he raised his hand and yelled out, "Here" since Mr. Horatio was hard of hearing, which was kind of funny given this was their Human Health class. Taking advantage of the open line of unexpected communication, Zach asked Everett, "Er, um, can I talk to you after class?"

Everett shrugged his amazing shoulders. "Yeah. We'll walk to physics lab together." Another amazing thing about Everett—he was wicked smart. He was in almost all of Zach's classes, and often challenged their physics teacher with thoughtful questions. Today in lab they were supposed to finish their in-class projects demonstrating Newton's Laws of Motion.

"Gr...great. Um, er, thanks."

When Mr. Horatio called out Everett's name, he waved at their teacher, which made the whole class laugh.

***

Everett

Zach Ellis was a hard one to figure. Yeah, the geek thing was as obvious as his round tortoiseshell glasses, but the guy who was ultra-confident academically, was an award-winning science whiz, and seemed pretty together—he dressed like a regular high schooler, no retro plastic pocket holder—was painfully shy around Everett. Since he didn't get the gay vibe off the cute geek, Everett figured Zach was more comfortable with concepts than people. Though, he seemed pretty loose on the baseball field, but he sucked at soccer.

From day one—and initially, Everett had no fuckin' idea why— he'd wanted to kiss Zach. Sure, there was something about his long, lean body that appealed to him. And yeah, those big hazel eyes behind those enormous glasses were captivating in a *I-want-you* way. They seemed to see right into his soul when Zach glanced over at him. Which was often. But what got him the most was Zach was nice to everyone, even when they weren't nice to him. He wasn't all goody-goody glowing with radiance, but he was even-tempered and patient. To someone who grew up with people who barked out orders even about breakfast cereal, Zach's calm demeanor held a real, meaningful attraction. Everett thought Zach might have a thing for him, but again, no gay vibe. Too bad, really. Everett would've liked his first kiss to be with someone of substance.

Okay. Truth time. Everett Granville Montgomery had never fucked anyone, gotten fucked by anyone, had a blowjob, given a blowjob, touched another guy's dick, had his dick touched by another guy, and he'd never been kissed by a guy. Yeah, he threw off the experienced and doing it often thing, but it was all an act to keep his hustler shit real.

After class, he waited for Zach in the hall, and when he bumped into Everett, red streaks washed over his olive tone cheeks. Huh. Maybe he did have a thing for him.

"Sorry," Zach muttered.

"It's cool, man." Everett started walking and Zach fell in pace with him. He had long legs, and was probably only two or three inches shorter than Everett, and wouldn't that make kissing him easy? Fucking hell. He had to hold his shit together. "What'dya want to talk to me about?"

"Well," Zach lowered his deep voice—another thing that turned Everett on. "I don't want to insult you."

This guy. "Yeah. I don't want you to insult me either." Zach blanched. "Spit it out, Einstein."

The moniker made Zach smile. And *fuck me*. It dazzled. All straight strong teeth and a dimple in his left cheek. Oh yeah, Everett wanted to kiss the shit out of Zach Ellis. "Um, er, I want to talk to you about going out on a date."

If he didn't think it would look uncool, Everett would've stopped in the middle of the hall and banged on his ear to make sure he'd heard right. Instead, he dipped his head and asked, "Are you asking me out?" Zach spluttered, coughed, and looked like he was going to choke both literally and figuratively. Everett wasn't going to give him a chance to backtrack. "I accept. I'll pick you up on Friday night at seven." Zach's big hazel eyes widened to the size of lemon slices. "Give me your phone." Zach looked down at his hand as if the phone would magically appear, shook his head real fast, and then like an automaton, he reached into his back pocket and handed Everett his cell. He sent himself a text, then handed the phone back to Zach. "That's me. Text your address and what kind of food you like. We're going to dinner."

***

Zach

What the hell just happened? He was sure he'd said the right words in the correct order to make Everett understand Zach meant Everett was going to find him someone *else* to go out on a date with. How did it get tripped up on his tongue so it sounded like Zach was asking Everett out? Good thing they'd reached the physics lab or Zach would've had to run to the bathroom and flush himself down the toilet. Yes, he knew it wasn't physically possible, but metaphorically speaking, it would've been an excellent disappearing act.

Everett went across the room to his lab station and began working with his lab partner, Viviana Lopez, who was math brainiac. Word was, she expected an early admission letter from Yale.

Zach looked to his left and saw his lab partner, Ben Kapur, wasn't there. A mental sigh of relief. Not about Ben. Zach had known him since the sixth grade. They were friends. But without Ben here, Zach didn't have to talk. He could channel all his energy and focus into finishing his project. He needed to concentrate on something that took up some brain space. Anything to take his mind off getting into the sexy as hell Corvette with the sexy as sin, Everett Montgomery.

Distracting himself with Sir Isaac lasted until the bell rang, and then Zach had never moved faster in his life. After he'd stowed the project and checked out on his iPad, he darted into the hall and cut through the throng in the central courtyard to get to his English Lit class. One of the two classes he had without Everett.

Unlike the stereotypes some "experts" promulgated about right brain people versus left brain people's likes and aptitudes, Zach enjoyed losing himself in Geoffrey Chaucer's *Canterbury Tales* written in Middle English poem and prose. He wasn't sure he understood all of it as in depth as the students whose future lay in such study, but he liked learning about things that'd had a global impact.

Ms. Pruitt, their teacher, was British and was an enthusiastic supporter of all things literature, but was a bit frozen in the Middle English period. Zach was looking forward to the Renaissance and its more sumptuous take on life. And that single thought sent him spiraling down a familiar rabbit hole where he'd spent long hours ruminating over all the delectable parts of Everett's body he'd like to get to know personally. *Oh no.* Not in the middle of "The Wife of Bath's Tale." As if Zach needed to add lust to a lusty story.

Somehow, he made it through English Lit without having a meltdown or embarrassing himself. He'd like to believe he was above succumbing to his body's hormonal overload, but he accepted his fate. He was a throbbing gland who'd had no outlet except his imagination and his hands. Thank god he had his own bathroom with a big shower.

Speaking of showers, he had PE next...with Everett. This particular six-week rotation of various sports was soccer. As with everything at this left of liberal private academy in the heart of Marin County, all PE activities were coed. Zach was fine with the Mia Hamm types who butted heads with the David Beckham wannabes. They kept the attention off Zach's ineptitude. Of course, Everett was as brilliant at soccer as he was at physics. And yes, he wore those soccer shorts like the manufacturer had made them with Everett's thighs in mind.

When Zach looked to his right, he gulped. Those unbelievably rock-solid thighs were right next to him. Everett was opening the locker beside Zach's when he said, "Hey" in his raspy voice. Damn. Why did everything about him have to be so friggin' sexy?

Zach figured he had to man up at least a little if he was going to make it through an entire evening with sex on a thick stick as his date. He raised his head and looked directly into Everett's unusual eyes. The irises seemed to have copper spikes overlaying a light brown background. "Hey. Um, how was Chinese class?" Such a sap letting on he knew where Everett was when they weren't in class together.

"It's all Greek to me," Everett deadpanned wearing his wicked grin.

Zach smiled. He couldn't help himself. And at what he saw, his smile got wider. Everett seemed...enthralled. His grin had morphed into a soft smile, and his eyelids lowered as his gaze seemed to focus on Zach's left cheek. He lifted his hand to touch where Everett was staring and realized it was the spot where his dimple was when he smiled. So he did it again and watched in utter shock as Everett blinked really slowly, twice. His hooded eyes seemed to be promising Zach he'd get to live out every fantasy he'd ever had about Everett.

As Zach was leaning forward to do who knew what since his body moved without checking in with his brain, Eli Sumptner banged into him, propelling Zach into Everett's body. His thick strong arms wrapped around Zach, keeping them both from crashing onto the wooden bench behind them. When Eli turned around and muttered, "Sorry" before he shuffled away, Everett kept hold of Zach even though they weren't in any danger of falling. Well, okay, Zach had fallen a while ago, and his body was conveying the message loud and clear against one of Everett's amazing thighs.

Everett leaned his head down a fraction to whisper in Zach's ear, "Hold that thought until Friday night, Einstein."

Before Zach knew what he was doing, he leaned his head against Everett's shoulder and muttered, "Two days seems like a lifetime away." At this juncture, there was no point in denying how he felt. His impossibly hard dick was doing all the talking for him.

"Yeah," Everett breathed the word into Zach's neck.

Slowly, they moved apart and Zach looked up to see Everett licking his lips as he adjusted the bulge in his body-hugging black jeans.

Zach had to close his eyes and think of cleaning up the dog shit in the backyard to stop himself from coming in his pants.

***

Everett

Keeping himself from busting his nut had taken self-control he never knew he had. That fuckin' dimple did him in. And Zach's long thick hard-on pressing against his thigh was almost too much to bear. He knew he was attracted to Zach, but he hadn't expected to be damn near mesmerized by his scent. When Everett had pressed his nose underneath Zach's thick auburn hair, he smelled like sex. Not that Everett really knew what sex smelled like, but the musty sort of earthy scent must be what people gave off when they were dancing between the sheets.

All these thoughts about Zach were not conducive to driving on the 580 as Everett headed home to Benecia. His mother was stationed at Travis Air Force Base, and she chose to live in Benecia since it was about halfway between his school in San Rafael and the base. It meant he commuted on a busy corridor every day—the traffic especially shitty in the afternoon. He wished he lived closer to Zach so they could hang out after school, but part of the bargain he'd made with his mom was she'd pay through the nose for the private school tuition, but he had to be home by 5 pm every school day. Since classes got out at 3:10 pm, and on a good day, it took him an hour to get home, plus he had to handle his side hustle orders, making it in the door by five was often a skin of his teeth kind of thing. His mom got home between 4 and 4:30, so there was no fudging his arrival time.

He'd be eighteen at the end of February, and technically he wouldn't have to obey his Lieutenant Colonel mother who commanded a unit at the David Grant USAF Medical Center. But their relationship had been strained by her deployments, and he wanted to spend as much time with her as he could.

Figuring he'd be able to text and talk to Zach now that he had his number, it'd have to be enough until Friday night. Detouring to his favorite pawn shop in El Cerrito, whose owner always had a line on something, Everett parked around back and ducked in through the back door. Everyone thought his hustle was illegal, criminal, and dangerous. He didn't disabuse them of their beliefs. It added to his rep, and drove up the prices for his services. These kids grew up posh. They couldn't tell the difference between street and someone playin' street, and Everett was definitely playin' street.

Today's find wasn't a hard ask. Bethany Issacs was trying to impress her new boyfriend who was a sophomore at San Francisco State. Chick was tippin' on this asshole's dick—she wanted a deal on a Rolex. He told her to go on eBay, but she insisted on getting the box and the papers even though he explained it was going to cost her almost as much a new one. She didn't even blink when she wrote the model number on the envelope stuffed full of Benjamins she'd pushed into his hand. Fidiot girl. Dude's gonna take the gift and forget she was alive. Yeah, cynical, but he'd met a lot of people in different parts of the world over the years, and no matter the country or the culture, people were selfish and could be abuse-level cruel.

Ten minutes later, he walked out with exactly what Bethany had asked for, got in his car and headed home.

At four minutes to five, he walked into the house through the garage, dumping him into the laundry room. Through the doorway separating the laundry room from the kitchen, he heard his mother humming to a Whitney Houston song, and he noticed something smelled really good. He smiled and shook his head. His mother's cooking was hit and miss at best. He'd bet his take on the Rolex, she'd ordered in.

When he walked into the kitchen, she turned around holding up chopsticks still in their little white packets. "Chinese?" he asked as he bent down to kiss her on the cheek.

She nodded. "Double Lotus Palace. I love their vegetable fried rice." The word "love" was stretched into three syllables as was her way. Having grown up in New Orleans, she had a rich and colorful way of speaking. A true Creole, she had bright blue eyes from her French ancestors, and dusky brown skin from her Afro-Caribbean heritage. His dad was Puerto Rican and Black, and had grown up in Harlem, which made Everett a little of everything. His grandmother used to say, "Baby, you're a true chile of the world."

After he and his mom had brought over plates and all the little white and red boxes filled with food, they sat at the kitchen table and began their ritual of talking about their day. His mother shared as much as she was able, and he had no problem telling her pretty much everything. "Got a date Friday night," he said around his savory noodles.

"Really? How wonderful. Tell me about him." He'd come out to his parents, who still did family Christmas when their schedules allowed, the December before his fourteenth birthday. They'd paused cleaning up wrapping paper, looked at each other for a brief moment, and then asked if he wanted to talk about it. He'd shook his head, they shrugged, and that was the extent of it.

"Well, I've been sorta crushing on him since school started." He bit into a greasy eggroll and nearly moaned before he swallowed. "His name is Zach, and he's Einstein brilliant. Most of all though, he's a good human."

"This Zach crushing on you?" she asked in her momma bear tone.

He smiled. "Yeah. Big time. But he's shy so it took him a minute." He finished off the eggroll. "He's all in now."

"That's good. Don't stay out past midnight 'kay?" He scrunched his face, and she laughed. "Humor your mother."

"A little give, mom. Let's say one."

She tilted her head to the left, and then sighed. "One. But not a minute later."

***

Zach

His mother couldn't boil water, but his father could've been a gourmet chef. They didn't have elaborate meals every night, but they ate tasty food all the time. Tonight, his father dove into his Italian bag of tricks and made *carciofi alla Guidia*, artichokes Jewish style, along with tagliatelle with sauteed mushrooms. His father's mother was from an old family of Italian Jews whose last name was Servi. According to historians, *servi*, which meant servants in Italian, were the Temple servants who were known as Levis in Hebrew. Apparently, around two thousand years ago, they were brought to Italy as slaves by Emperor Titus after he'd ransacked Israel.

As his mother was serving the salad, Zach said, "I have a date Friday night." Then he pulled off a hunk of homemade *ciabatta* and dipped it in a small pool of olive oil and balsamic vinegar on his bread plate.

"That's great, honey. Do we know him?" He'd been in school with most of his classmates since kindergarten, which was about the time he knew he was gay. According to his parents, who'd he told as a point of information when he was about eleven, they'd known since he was around four or five. They were the kind of people who didn't believe in making a big deal about things unless it was absolutely required. Him being gay was not a big deal.

"Nope," he answered, his fork halfway to his mouth. "He's new." After he chewed and swallowed a huge wedge of a homegrown heirloom tomato, he shared, "You'll meet him. He's picking me up here."

"Looking forward to it," his father said as he forked up some *carciofi alla Guidia."*

***

Everett

Thursday and Friday were torture. Almost every class with Zach, lunch with Zach, talking to Zach, texting with Zach, but he was never alone with Zach. Yeah, he'd caught whiffs of his musky scent, and watched as Zach ran his fingers through his hair when he was working out a problem, then walked into the hallway totally unconcerned with how he looked. They'd agreed, during PE they wouldn't change in front of each other. Zach was four rows of lockers away from Everett. Neither of them wanted to put on the totally erect woody show for their classmates. When they walked down the halls between classes they didn't hold hands. Not because the school gave a shit, or because they cared what anyone would say, but because they were burning for each other and the slightest touch would've set off a four-alarmer.

Friday at lunch Zach plopped onto the bench too close to Everett and their bodies brushed from shoulder to thigh. He grabbed Zach's hand under the table and squeezed. Hard. Hoping the pain distracted them enough to get through the rest of the day without imploding.

He'd barely made it through last period, and he knew if he didn't do something before their date tonight, they'd never make it to the Persian restaurant Zach wanted to go to.

E: Meet me by my car after your last class.
Z: Okay. Something wrong?
E: No.
Z: CUL

He was leaning against the passenger door when he saw Zach's long-limbed stride head toward the Vette. It took everything in him to force his body to move around to the driver's side, get in and start the car.

Zach got in, buckled up, and then asked, "Are you all right?"

He shook his head, but wouldn't look at Zach. "I will be in about fifteen minutes."

"Do I want to know why?"

Grinding his back teeth, he turned to look at the guy who was making him fuckin' crazy with need and said, "You know why."

Zach's eyes widened in that way he had, making him look even more adorable. He gulped and nodded.

Everett eased out the parking lot, and managed to get past the row of fidiot drivers before he let the Vette loose. The tires ate up the road as he drove them to McNears Beach. Five miles, but fifteen long fuckin' minutes on Point San Pedro Road, they rode in silence, as if words would cause them to combust.

Finally, he pulled into McNears and drove down the access road to the parking lot. He jumped out, popped the trunk, grabbed his and Zach's knapsacks and threw them in, then slammed it shut. Before Zach could say a word, Everett grabbed his hand and walked them into the woods. When he was sure no one was around, he back Zach against a large tree, released his hand and laid his palms on either side of Zach's head. The rough wood dug into his skin, but he didn't care.

Zach's lips ticked up into a small smile, and he took off his glasses and went to stuff them in his front pocket, then he must've thought the better of it and tossed them a few feet away.

"If I don't kiss you right now, I'm going to—"

He didn't get out another word. Zach's soft, lush lips landed on his and... Oh yeah. This was so worth waiting for. This was everything. Zach ran his tongue along the seam of Everett's mouth and as he opened, Zach whispered against his lips, "Explode."

Through his smile, he welcomed Zach's hot tongue as it glided and tangled with his, the incredible sensations made his stomach drop, his toes curl, and his dick throb against the zipper of his jeans. He grabbed Zach's face and took the kiss deeper, dueling tongues and racing pulses. He could feel Zach's heart beating against his, their chests aligned, their hips grinding in sync, their moans deep and soulful. He shifted his head, and Zach wrapped his arms around his back and then hooked his hands over Everett's shoulder. He snugged their groins closer together until not a wisp of air was between them.

And they kept kissing, giving and taking, mapping each other's mouths until the landscape became an indelible part of him.

Slowly, he lifted his head and waited until Zach looked up. Those beautiful hazel eyes were lit from within, and he understood the feeling. Nothing had ever felt more right than kissing Zach.

"Now I can breathe," he whispered before he kissed Zach's brow. "If I didn't taste you before we went to dinner, I knew we were never going to make it."

"You realize we're plastered together," Zach's voice was husky and deeper than usual.

"Complaining?"

Zach shook his head. "Simply noting we haven't let go of each other."

Before he could stop himself from saying it, the words slipped out of Everett's mouth. "I don't think I'm ever going to let you go."

Zach smiled and that wonderful dimple popped out. Everett leaned in to kiss it, then trailed his lips over Zach's cheek, down to his jaw, and over to the damp musky spot beneath his ear.

Everett wanted to bathe in Zach's earthy scent and rubbed his nose against Zach's neck, breathing him in deeply until the smell of him settled in Everett's cells. He wanted to access that scent whenever he needed it to remind himself Zach was his, and he intended to keep him.

"Want to walk along the beach, or are we going to stay glued together for another couple of hours?"

"I don't mind staying glued together," he muttered into Zach's neck as he ran his fingers through Zach's thick hair.

"Well, I do."

Everett jerked his head back to check if Zach was serious, but he couldn't read him. "Uh, what the fuck?"

"Exactly," Zach said.

Everett thought he understood, but he wanted clarification since he'd never felt more at one with another human being than he did right now. "You want to—"

"Yes, and no. More yes, but I know no is the better answer."

Everett chuckled. "Okay, Einstein, hit me."

"Here's the thing, and I know I'm not supposed to reveal this stuff, but I figure since we can't seem to separate, I'm not exactly broadcasting a news flash." Everett raised his brows in the hopes Zach would get to the point. Although, listening to whatever he had to say was amusing or truly amazing. "I've... Well shit, this is embarrassing after all." Everett blinked rapidly to encourage Zach to continue. "Er, um... Oh, what the hell. I've fantasized about what it would be like to be with you. You know. *Be* with you. Kiss you, and," he swiveled his hips and their hard cocks rubbed against each other through the fabric of their jeans, "everything else. I want it so bad, some days it seems like it's all I can think about. Now that we're, you know..."

"Together."

"Uh-huh. Together. I don't want us to fuck this up by fucking too soon." Everett waited to hear if there was more. "Am I making sense?"

Everett cupped Zach's face. "Do I want to fuck your brains out until you're hoarse from screaming my name? Hell yeah. But I'm not going anywhere, and as much as my dick is dancing in my pants to get to yours, I know it's better to wait. Anticipation is a good kind of torture, and we need time to lay the groundwork. You're not some quick fuck and adios, baby. You're my Zach and I'm pretty sure I'm going to keep you."

***

Zach

Z: I hate my roommate. He's a slob. He snores, and he farts in his sleep. When I wake up, it smells like I'm living inside a toilet bowl.

E: Hahahahaahha. That's what you get for going to MIT, home of the super geeks. You're too cool to put up with those low-lifers.

Z: Is this you lamenting?

E: I'm pretty sure I made it clear I hated being away from you.

Z: Of the two of us, I should've known you'd be the drama queen. You're 3.5 hours away by train. You're at Columbia for fuck's sake. An Ivy. I'll see you Saturday.

Zach waited the requisite three minutes for Everett to decide if he was going to be petulant or a smartass. Either way worked for Zach. The love of his life was a bossy prima donna who had too much swagger for a dude with such a big brain. And yes, a big dick.

After they'd finally pulled away from each other that fantastic day they'd first kissed and kissed until Everett's lips were red and pouty, they held hands, walked along the beach, and talked. In all they'd said, the most important thing was they'd agreed they wanted to make what they had work, and decided to wait while they got to know "them" before they fucked each other stupid.

Zach had been surprised Everett was an inexperienced as he was, but there was something about it being the first time for both of them that made it sweeter. Over the course of the fall semester, they'd spent as much time together as they could, and they *learned* each other. It turned out, Everett was neat freak, Zach had a temper, and neither could stay angry with the other for more than a couple hours. Zach was practical and steady, and, for obvious reasons, Everett had some abandonment issues he needed to work through.

On February twenty-third, Zach gave himself to Everett for his birthday. Given his dramatic nature, Everett was better at telling the story, but Zach would remember that night as long as he lived. Nothing was better than acting out his fantasies with the man who loved him.

E: I'm leaving on Friday on the 6 pm Acela. I'll be in Back Bay a little past 9:30.

Z: What about your paper?

E: I'll finish it tomorrow and turn it in Friday afternoon.

Z: In other words, you're pulling an all-nighter.

E: I'm young, and I'll get some shut-eye on the train. Life's too short to sleep alone.

Z: I'll call the hotel and change the reservation. TTYT. I gotta hit the lab.

***

Everett

Zach had wanted him to go to MIT. But he knew being there would cramp Zach's style. Not in the fuck-boy kind of way, but in the attention to his work and his studies way, which was far more important. Everett wasn't kidding when he called him Einstein. Zach was going to do great things with his brain, and he needed to focus on getting there. But Zach was a nurturer. He came from a long line of nurturers, and Everett refused to let him get distracted with taking care of his man when he needed to keep his eye on the ball.

Rolling back the mental vid to their first date, Everett knew Zach was it for him, and he had to make sure Zach stayed the course. Of the two of them, Zach's contributions to the world would matter more. Not that Everett wasn't important. He had a big enough ego to know he would do great things, but Zach and what he could accomplish was way more important.

After they'd unlocked their bodies, they'd walked along the beach and made promises. So far, they'd kept all of them. Did he want to jump Zach's bones every day of fall semester? Ah, yeah. But they went slow. Lots of kissing and ass grabbing. Some serious dry humping—*denim is not a forgiving material*—and they got outrageously good at phone sex. Between them, they must've come two hundred times from talking about what they'd do before they did it.

Zach had applied for early acceptance to MIT and got his thumbs-up letter in mid- December. They celebrated privately on New Year's Eve, and even though it was his night, he gave Everett his first blow job. For real, Zach could give Dyson a run for their money. Since Everett knew he was Zach's first, he had to ask where Zach had learned to do all that shit that made his balls empty so hard and for so long he thought he was going to pass out. Zach's answer: research. Lots and lots of gay porn before he put his luscious lips around Everett's cock. Since he'd had a built-in professor, Everett let Zach tell him what he liked and how Everett was supposed to go about doing it. Van Halen had it right: *I was hot for teacher*.

Best birthday of Everett's life: his eighteenth. Zach had the whole night planned. They went into San Francisco and had and early dinner in China Town. Yeah, Zach learned real quick Chinese food was an obsession. Then they went to the Orpheum Theater to see *Hamilton*, and after they walked only a few blocks to the Hotel Zetta where they learned their bodies were completely compatible. Not that Everett had any doubts. The thing about that night? He didn't fuck Zach until his ears bled. They went slow, and tender, and when he entered Zach's body, which felt like heaven on earth, tears ran down Everett's cheeks: how lucky was he at such a young age to have found the love of his life.

The summer between high school graduation and their freshman year at college, they spent in the Vette seeing the country. Yeah, they fucked in fancy hotels and cheap motels, and tried to act out gay porn as they were watching it. They took river raft rides, visited National Parks, and ate all kinds of food, some of it fuckin' awful.

They spent a few days in New Orleans with Everett's people, and drove along the eastern seaboard, stopping at empty beaches where they loved each other until the sun disappeared from the sky.

Now, in the middle of their last semester of college, they'd become familiar figures on the Acela train between Boston and NYC, and had visited more hotels in both cities than Frommer's. Zach was continuing on at MIT to get his PhD, and Everett had a surprise for his man. This time they were going uptown all the way. Everett had booked them in at The Pierre hotel. But that wasn't his surprise.

He met Zach at Penn Station and saw right away: Zach didn't feel well. "What the fuck, Einstein?" he asked as he hugged him, then slung his arm over Zach's shoulder.

"It's nothing. I must have a stomach bug or something."

"Bullshit." They stepped outside and he hailed a cab, then told the driver to take them to The Pierre. He waited until after they were checked in and were in their room before he sat Zach on the edge of the bed and started to examine him. "Sit still," he grumbled when Zach kept batting away his hands.

"I want to get laid, and you're playing *The Good Doctor*."

He stopped for a minute, got the envelope out of his jacket pocket and pushed it into Zach's hand. "Lie back and let me take a look at your stomach."

"I'm down with the lie back part, but you're a bit high geographically if you're interested in my stomach." Zach turned the envelope over in his hand and asked, "What's this?"

"Open it."

"While I'm lying down and you're pushing on my... Ow. Stop it. That hurts."

"Asshole. It's not supposed to hurt. It's your appendix. C'mon." He helped Zach sit up. "Can you walk?"

"For fuck's sake, of course I can walk." But when Zach went to stand, he plopped back down on the edge of the bed, and his olive toned skin blanched white.

"Lie down." This time Zach did what he was told. "I'm going to press lightly. I promise not to hurt you, but I'm feeling for hot spots."

"Um, okay. But why?"

"I think your appendix has ruptured and you're bleeding internally."

"Well, shit," Zach muttered. "I guess this means I'm not getting laid this weekend."

Everett wasn't taking any chances. He wasn't going to make Zach go downstairs upright. If he'd guessed correctly, Zach needed immediate medical attention. He called 911. Ten minutes later a paramedic and an EMT arrived and they took Zach to Lennox Hill Hospital where he had an emergency appendectomy.

Everett sat next to Zach's bed waiting for him to come to. He'd been brought into his room only a few minutes ago after spending about a half hour in recovery. The surgeon had spoken to Everett—he'd lied and said Zach was his husband, otherwise they wouldn't've told him jack-shit—and confirmed Everett's diagnosis. The appendix had ruptured, but hadn't presented any other complications than warranting its removal. They were pumping Zach full of antibiotics to prevent infection, and were going to keep him for no more than forty-eight hours as long as he remained infection free. At-home recovery would probably take a little more than two weeks.

Everett pressed his head against Zach's hand and drew in a deep breath. After this scare from hell, he saw no reason for them to wait. This summer they were getting married. He wasn't going to take no for an answer. Zach began to stir and Everett leaned forward, pushing Zach's thick auburn hair off his forehead. "Hey," he said softly when Zach's eyes fluttered open.

"Hey," Zach whispered. "Does this mean I can't get pregnant?"

"Asshole." Everett leaned forward and kissed Zach lightly on the mouth. Then he told him everything the surgeon had said, and how he'd called their families and told everyone what happened and that Zach was all right.

"Looks like I'm staying with you for a couple of weeks, huh?" Zach took another ice cube Everett fed him from a stupid small plastic cup with a stupid white plastic spoon.

"Yeah. I'm guessing you brought your laptop."

"Ah-huh."

"Anything you need shipped down from Boston?"

"Not that I can think of right now." Zach closed his eyes. He was drifting off to sleep. "Everything should be in the laptop," he mumbled.

When he woke again a couple hours later, he seemed more alert. "Hey. What was in the envelope?"

Everett squeezed his hand gently. "It can wait."

"I know you. Remember. We met in high school"

"And you call me a drama queen."

"C'mon, Ev. Tell me. It's something important. What's in the envelope?"

"I got into Tuft's medical school."

"Holy shit." Zach managed to squeeze Everett's fingers. "We can finally live together."

Oh, Einstein, we're going to be more than living together.

***

Zach

He couldn't believe everyone came. Aunts and uncles from Italy. Cousins from Israel. Everett's great auntie from Puerto Rico, two cousins and their kids from New York City, and *everyone* from New Orleans. All of them and the California families stuffed into folding chairs—nice ones because his mother wouldn't allow anything less—in his parent's backyard.

To be fair, the yard was nearly two acres so between the ceremony area and the huge reception tent, it wasn't as if they were cramped and crowded. Busy, the backyard was filled with noisy, happy people who had plenty of room to wander.

Which was what his soon-to-be husband was doing, wandering the perimeter. Zach knew Everett wasn't nervous about getting married. He'd been the one who insisted they did this summer. Zach knew the whole ruptured appendix debacle had spawned the proposal. Which worked for him. He'd never wanted anyone but Everett, and would always want only Everett. Zach figured his man was making promises to himself. Something he did to keep his goals on target. Today, his goals were probably to be a good and loving husband who would stay married to Zach until they drew their last breaths.

Marjorie—Colonel Montgomery, she'd been promoted a couple of years back—sat next to Zach in the front row. "He's doing his promise thing, huh?"

"Yep. We're waiting on him to circle back to get this party started."

"Thank you," she said softly as she patted his arm.

Zach blinked. "For what?"

"For loving my son, whose eyes light up every time you walk into a room."

Okay. As compliments go from your mother-in-law-to-be, that was as good as it gets. "Well, don't tell anyone, but he makes my heart do somersaults too."

"Sorry, Zach, but I think your secret's out." She turned her head and Zach followed her line of sight. "Here he comes now. I'll go get his father."

Fifteen minutes later they were standing in front of the rabbi who'd bar-mitzvahed Zach. Religion meant nothing to Everett and it was important to Zach so Everett shrugged and said, "Yeah, we're Jewish" and that was it.

Now, they were saying their vows.

After they both stepped on glasses wrapped in linen napkins and broke the crystal into pieces, and after everyone yelled "Mazel Tov," Everette leaned down and kissed Zach.

And just like the first time, Zach didn't let go.

ABOUT THE AUTHORS

M. Tasia

M. Tasia is a M/M romance author who lives in Ontario, Canada. She's is a dedicated people watcher, lover of romance novels, 80's rock, and happily-ever-afters (once the MCs are put through their paces, of course), who grew up with a love of reading. She's a firm believer that everyone deserves to have love, excitement, and crazy hot romance in their lives. Love should be celebrated and shared.

CONNECT WITH M.:
mtasiabooks.com
IG: @m.tasia.author
twitter: @mtasiaauthor
FB: mtasiabooks

Susan Mac Nicol

The 'Official' stuff

Susan writes steamy, sexy, and fun contemporary romance stories, some suspenseful, some gritty and dark, and she hopes, always entertaining. She's also Editor-in-Chief at Divine Magazine, an online LGBTQ e-zine, and a member of The Society of Authors, the Writers Guild of Great Britain, and the Authors Guild in the U.S.

Susan is also an award-winning screenplay writer, with scripts based on two of her own published works. *Sight Unseen* has garnered no less than five awards to date, and her TV pilot, *Reel Life*, based on her debut novel, *Cassandra by Starlight*, was also a winner at the Oaxaca Film Fest.

The 'Unofficial' stuff

Susan loves going to the theatre, live music concerts (especially if it's her man-crush Adam Lambert), walks in the countryside, a good G and T, lazing away afternoons reading a good book, and watching re-runs of *Silent Witness*.

Her chequered past includes stories like being mistaken for a prostitute in the city of Johannesburg, being chased by a rhino on a dusty Kenyan road, getting kicked out of a youth club for being a bad influence (she encouraged free thinking), and having an aunt who was engaged to Cliff Richard.

CONNECT WITH SUSAN:
website: authorsusanmacnicol.com
IG: @susiemax77
twitter: @SusanMacNicol7
linkedin: susanmacnicol
FB: Author-Susan-Mac-Nicol

Emily Mims

The author of over forty romance novels, Emily Mims combined her writing career with a career in public education until leaving the classroom to write full time. The mother of two sons, she and her husband split their time between central Texas, eastern Tennessee, and overseas visiting their kids and grandchildren. For relaxation Emily plays the piano, organ, dulcimer, and ukulele for two different performing groups, and even sings a little. She says, "I love to write romances because I believe in them. Romance happened to me and it can happen to any woman—if she'll just let it."

CONNECT WITH EMILY:
website: emilymims.com
IG: @mims_emily
twitter: @emilymimsauthor
FB: emily.mims.756

Kitty Bardot

Kitty Bardot juggles a life full of excitement and love. By day, she's a chef with her own catering company, by night she puts ten years of burlesque experience to use in various venues in the Quad Cities. She writes from her country home not far from the Mississippi River, enjoying every moment with her husband and their three children. Currently, she is working on her next Burlesque River story.

CONNECT WITH KITTY:
website: kittybardot.net
IG: @ktbardot
twitter: @KittyBardot
FB: Kitty-Bardot-312641412082507

Elle Wright

Elle Wright has been writing stories since she was a child, which led her to a career in journalism. She enjoys reporting life as much as making up a world she can control. She lives on the east coast of the United States where most of her large, noisy family resides. When she isn't in front of her computer, she loves to travel, garden, hang out with her dogs, and take in the brisk sea air that she's told is supposed to help calm her. She's been testing that theory for a while now.

CONNECT WITH ELLE:
twitter: @ElleWright18
IG: @Elle_Wright_Writes
FB: elle.wright.1460

2**www.BOROUGHSPUBLISHINGGROUP.com**

If you enjoyed this book, please write a review. Our authors appreciate the feedback, and it helps future readers find books they love. We welcome your comments and invite you to send them to info@boroughspublishinggroup.com. Follow us on Facebook, Twitter and Instagram, and be sure to sign up for our newsletter for surprises and new releases from your favorite authors.

Are you an aspiring writer? Check out www.boroughspublishinggroup.com/submit and see if we can help you make your dreams come true.

www.ingramcontent.com/pod-product-compliance
Lightning Source LLC
Chambersburg PA
CBHW071401170626
46811CB00003B/1217